"An engrossing literary love letter. Only a true believer could craft a work of such relevance and heart, and every facet of this novel, from chapter headings designed as censored books to finely etched characters and witty teen-speak dialogue, proves this author's worth as a champion of literature. A timely read that will ultimately prove timeless." —*KIRKUS REVIEWS* (starred review)

"Wry, thought-provoking, rebellious, and predicated on the belief that the right book changes everything. The well-told story of a frustrated teen fighting for social justice will be a hit with young people." —*SLJ*

"In this thought-provoking novel, Connis tackles themes of censorship, resistance, and the power of the written word through a diverse cast of characters, bold prose, and humor that breaks up even the darkest moments." —*ALA BOOKLIST*

"*Suggested Reading* is a beautiful reminder that there is nothing simple about loving a book. I suggest you read it."

—DAVID ARNOLD, *New York Times* bestselling
author of *Mosquitoland*

"Audiences will fall in love with this genuine and funny exploration of reading as an act of resistance."

—RANDY RIBAY, author of *After the Shot Drops*
and the National Book Award finalist *Patron Saints of Nothing*

"Thought-provoking and impossible to put down."

—C. J. REDWINE, *New York Times* bestselling author

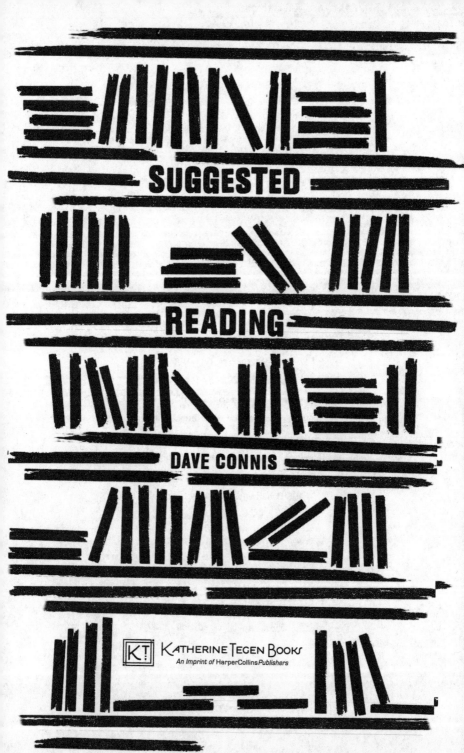

# SUGGESTED

# READING

## DAVE CONNIS

**KT** KATHERINE TEGEN BOOKS
*An Imprint of HarperCollins Publishers*

Katherine Tegen Books is an imprint of HarperCollins Publishers.

Suggested Reading

ISBN 978-0-06-268526-1

Typography by David Curtis

20 21 22 23 24   PC/LSCH   10 9 8 7 6 5 4 3 2 1

❖

First paperback edition, 2020

*To Clara*

*For being someone I'm honored (and proud) to name main characters after*

*Do I dare disturb the universe?*

—Robert Cormier, *The Chocolate War* . . . sort of.

More like T. S. Eliot if we really want to get technical.

## THE ANNUAL EVANS HIGHLIGHTER ALL-NIGHTER

Four years.

48 months.

1,461 days.

35,064 hours.

2,103,840 minutes.

126,230,400 seconds.

That's how long I'd waited for the new book by my favorite author, Lukas Gebhardt: *Don't Tread on Me.*

To put it in perspective, I was graduating middle school when I read Lukas's last book, *A House of Wooden Windows.* That one I'd had signed by him. The gorgeous man took my breath away with his words on the daily, and the thrill of knowing I held a very real book-shaped *Don't*

*Tread on Me* in my hands made me question even getting out of my car and walking in my house before starting, but the pull of the couch was stronger than the pull of sitting in a running car. Shocking, I know.

I chanted, *"Don't Tread on Me, Don't Tread on Me, Don't Tread on Me,"* as I walked inside, fresh from the land of marvel and mischief, spells and superlatives, counter curses, cultures, love-baked digressions, rabbit-trail wisdom, symphonies of folly and fable, illumined reality, and glow-in-the-dark wonder: the local bookstore.

It was ten o'clock. There was nary an Evans parent in sight. Both in bed, for sure; they were early risers, which was the point. There were very few things I kept from my parents, but the Evans Highlighter All-Nighter tradition, which I'd held since freshman year of high school, was one of them. The Highlighter All-Nighter was the highest point of my rebellion. I stayed up on a school night—the first school night—to read a book and drink fruit juice out of a carton. On the Spectrum of Safety for Renegade Youths, I was unchartable. The highest of percentiles.

It was a silly secret, but it was a secret nonetheless.

Besides, regardless of tradition, I needed to read *DTOM*

anyway. My long-running book club—Queso . . . What Are We Reading Next?—was meeting in less than twenty-four hours to discuss the first few chapters of *DTOM*, and I needed to be ready to lead it. No, I didn't need to read the whole thing, but that wasn't the point, was it?

I pulled a carton of mango nectar, the official drink of EHAN, out of the fridge.

I cut up a block of cheddar cheese and put the slices on a plate filled with water crackers.

I walked into the living room, grabbed the orange highlighters out of my pockets (yellow highlighters are overrated), and stood them on their flat ends like pillars to hold up the time and night. Lighthouses to remind me of my direction when the gales of sleepiness came.

I plopped on the couch.

Ready.

Sixteen-year-old Levi lives in the neutral zone of the Second Civil War, on a farm harvesting cash crops for military rations, but when his town is swallowed into the borders of the Western Forces, he's shipped off to the front lines, leaving everything behind.

Seventeen-year-old Joss has never known anything but the Eastlands, Dixie. Born in a house on the Mason-Dixon line, he's been raised to fight for the restoration of a long-forgotten nation. His grandpa is a general; his dad, a high-ranking medic. And now he is a newly promoted second lieutenant.

In a meeting orchestrated by the bloody injustices of war, the boys are thrown together when they're forced to kill an innocent civilian. With nothing but the idea that there has to be something better, the boys run away. Traveling the Deserters' Corridor, the closely monitored northern path of the neutral zone, they stumble on an old limestone mining tunnel, where they build the first library without war-side bias since before the first gunshot was even fired, bringing together literature and cultural items from underground artifact dealers.

As they attempt to fuse the splintered world back together, Levi and Joss find themselves leading a new movement. With an army at their command, they become enemies of both sides of the war, and when the neutral zone is declared forfeit and new battle lines threaten to unravel everything they've worked for, they must decide if the library, and all it stands for, is worth their lives.

## THE BLURBS

"A balm for those brave enough to look for common ground during the Great Unrest."

—Colt Cax, author of the *New York Times* best seller *Strange Astrophysics*

"Lukas Gebhardt paints a poignant picture of the bleeding heart of America."

—Ishmael Aventu, author of *A Country for Thieves*

"Nothing like reading a classic book for the first time."

—Keri Limonhouse, author of *Goody Blu's Shoes*

**THE AUTHOR BIO ON THE BACK PAGE**

Lukas Gebhardt was born in Namibia and now resides in Houston, Texas. He received his doctorate in philosophy at Harvard University and now serves as a professor of philosophy at the University of Houston.

## FEELINGS, TIME, AND *DON'T TREAD ON ME*

**10:34 p.m.**

The cover: Design genius. A straight re-creation of the Don't Tread on Me flag. The only exception is that *Lukas Gebhardt* is inked into the diamond pattern on the snake's body. The snake looks less like clip art and more hand-sketched. Though I'm not sure why I think the original snake looked like clip art, considering it was designed in 1775. Which was back when clip art wasn't that advanced.

**10:35 p.m.**

The acknowledgments (I always read them first): disappointed. My name didn't show up once. I even read through a few more times to make sure.

**10:37–10:51 p.m.** | Pages 1–13

A civil war. A smart, compassionate boy fighting because he didn't know better. I'm already drowning in vicious heartbreak.

**10:52–11:08 p.m.** | Pages 13–34

Less engulfed by heartbreak. More engulfed by feelings in general. Such a dark world. Reminds me of *Fahrenheit 451*, but with more executions and less TV.

**11:08–11:53 p.m.** | Pages 34–66

Good.

Lord.

Lukas never disappoints. My highlighter highlights furious and frequent. Blocks of orange everywhere, like a game of page Tetris. Things like "And just like that, it came over me. I wasn't even a cog. I was a number on a clockface. I had no mass apart from the machine. Everything was *panem et circenses*, bread and circuses. The formula for a happy kingdom. Food and pleasure. Pleasure and food. As this was also my diet, this was my fear: If I somehow could comprehend how to leave this place,

I'd simply dissolve into the atmosphere. Particles in the wind."

**12:05–12:20 a.m.** | Pages 66–78

Terrified. Terrified. Terrified. I pace back and forth while reading. How had I lived without this book?

**12:20–12:24 a.m.** | Pages 78–80

What . . . ?

[MANGO NECTAR REFILL INTERMISSION]

**12:24–1:08 a.m.** | Pages 80–102

Still recovering from pages seventy-eight to eighty. Feeling guilty for getting more mango nectar because I feel like I'm playing into *panem et circenses*. Am I constantly in need of food and entertainment? I look at the plate of cheese. The new glass of mango nectar. I curl into myself. Will I disappear if I don't drink it? What am I made of? My God. The book made me question cheese. I mark my place with a bookmark and toss it on the table, staring at it as if it could kill me, and actually wondering if it might if I keep reading. Should I keep reading?

**1:09–2:06 a.m.** | Pages 102–200

Incredible. Haven't felt so invested in a revolution since *The Hunger Games*. Lukas, you have my bow.

**2:06–3:30 a.m.** | Pages 200–300

A hard weep is coming. I can feel it. I'm eating some cheese.

**3:30–4:53 a.m.** | Pages 300–488

Plate of cheese and crackers has been reduced to crumbs and, not coincidentally, I've been reduced to tears. Wow.

## PANEM ET CIRCENSES

*Let the wild rumpus start.*

—Maurice Sendak, *Where the Wild Things Are*

I was silent as I drove to Lupton Academy for my last first day of high school.

Normally, I'd listen to a morning-drive mix on my phone and mumble along with the words in an effort to feel like I had some musicality, but I couldn't. That was the cost of reading Lukas Gebhardt. He supplied words, but he demanded tears and being torn apart as payment.

I was wrecked. Undone. Shredded. My soul replaced with a tornado. Hurricane Clara. Category: Emotionally Distraught.

To be fair, I wasn't entirely sure how much having stayed up until five played into my wreckedness, but . . . I hadn't been wrecked by a book so hard since last year, which told me that *DTOM* was a contender for this year's Book That Changed My Life.

I turned onto Bottlers Avenue and passed under a wrought-iron archway that proclaimed I had, in fact, arrived at Lupton.

Bottlers Ave. was a straight shot into campus. No curves. No hills. Just a median separating the two sides of the road. I drove all the way to the end of it, past the stadium, the gym, and the maintenance building, and turned right into the faculty, staff, and senior parking lot.

One of Lupton's borders was an old train track, and the train track separated us from a fancy shopping center that also contained an Earth Foods Market. If you were anything but a senior, you had to park in a lot behind the Earth Foods and then walk across a little greenway connecting the lot to the paved path at the back of the school.

LA was notoriously cramped, which was actually how LA became the working name for Lupton Academy instead of Lupton. On the corner of two busy roads in the dead center of Chattanooga's North Shore, we'd expanded as far as we could without buying fifteen homes and a few businesses (junkyard, recycling center, and a self-storage place) behind us. These fifteen home and three business owners, also known as the Stringer and Peerless Alliance, a.k.a. SPA, knew we needed more room, hated the fact that LA was taking over their space, and had banded together to ask for a total of sixty-seven and a half million dollars for everything. Each of the fifteen 1950s two-bedroom, two-bath houses would get three and a half million, and each of the businesses would get five million. So we were in a gridlock. The school didn't have that sort of money to pay for expansion, and SPA wanted no less.

The campus had gotten lusher and greener over the summer and, as always, it looked beautiful. The parking-lot borders were filled with bushes and flowers, professionally cut and pruned within an inch of a *Better Homes and Gardens* photoshoot. Parking grid lines a fresh, pure white. Not a sliver of trash caught in the drainage inlets. The line of serviceberry trees separating LA from the SPA lands was a thick binding of pruned and intermingled leaves, a green fence whose leaves turned to fire in the fall.

I turned off the car and sat there for a while, drinking coffee and contemplating. I was early, and the campus was just starting to echo with the dewy cicada yawn of morning.

I sat and rehashed every molecule of *Don't Tread on Me*, from its beginning on a swaying cornfield to its end in the dark of a cave. I didn't want to speak too soon, but I thought it was one of my favorite books of all time. All its other merits aside, simply the concept of *panem et circenses* was like a pair of glasses I hadn't known I needed, and I was still adjusting to my new sense of sight.

I hopped out of the car and spun around, arms outstretched over the kingdom of the on-campus parking lot. And then it hit me. This was it. There'd be no more walking the underclass passage from the Earth Foods lot. This was my last year of volunteering for Mr. Caywell, LA's librarian.

It was the last first day I'd ever have.

So I took it all in.

I made myself listen to the birds chirping in the crepe myrtles across the lawn. I made myself smell my last first day's air. A crisp and fresh wet, and then an old and ancient dampness. The former a remnant of dew from the morning irrigation-sprinkler session, the latter a scent that occasionally floated in off the Tennessee River, which was only about a mile or so away. After that, I caught an urban cologne of gas mixed with the floral and savory smells of Earth Foods baking, cooking, stocking soaps and spices, and, thankfully, only a tiny hint of thick, sunbaked tarmac.

Suddenly it felt like it'd be a day where the wind would finally pick a color. Where the doors of LA, made of recycled Coke bottles, wouldn't gather fingerprints, where cars passing by on Cherokee Boulevard would sing songs instead of honk horns. And I knew:

It was going to be a beautiful day.

A beautiful year.

"'Let the wild rumpus start,'" I said to myself innocently, and sometimes I wonder: If I'd quoted something else, would my senior year have gone differently? Because, indeed, a wild rumpus did start.

## THE PROBABILITIES OF HAVING BEEN RAISED
## IN A BARN

It was only fifteen steps from one of the main stairwells of LA's flagship building, Lupton Hall, and my second home, LA's library. The library was housed in the front of Lupton Hall, the side of the building that most Chattanoogans would see if they were driving around the North Shore.

Light poured in from the outside through the colonial copper-topped dome, illuminating a wide-open space that Mr. Caywell and I had practically designed ourselves when the library underwent renovations my sophomore year. It was a clean space. Organized—well, except for the processing room, through a door behind Mr. Caywell's desk—but the white walls were devoid of posters, and I'd chop a patron if they even hinted at putting a poster anywhere but the community board.

A dark and rich walnut-brown stain coated chairs and shelves. Vintage black pendant lights—which used to hang in the factory the building had at one point been— hung above tables and the computer bar.

The space was dotted with plants. A lot of plants. Ficus. Fern. Fiddle-leaf fig. Peace lily. All donated by a student's parents who owned a big plant nursery on the outskirts of town. It was fancy for a library, but that was how Mr. Caywell and I liked it. Plants. Computers. Comfy chairs. Books. Coffee. Wi-Fi.

What else could you want?

There were, typically, two things you could count on from the library: overpopulation of state-mandated health-related brochures and Mr. Caywell sitting behind the desk at the back of the room. That morning, though, only the brochures were in their rightful place. Mr. Caywell was nowhere to be seen.

"Mr. Caywell?" I called, but nothing came back.

I walked behind the desk, then through the door to the processing room, a shallow but long rectangular cleaning closet overrun with book donations, old decorations, magazines, yellowing newspapers, and who knew what else. "Mr. Caywell?" I called again. "Are you here? We need to talk about Lukas's newest book. Hello?"

I spun on my heel and looked at his computer through the processing room door. It was on. His email was up.

I hadn't been raised in a barn. At least not to my recollection. I couldn't remember life before five years old, but I did know that I wasn't supposed to read other people's emails. On the Universal List of Things to Do to Avoid Being a Massive Trash Being, not reading other people's mail was number three, behind thou shall not murder and thou shall not give away spoilers for popular TV shows on social media.

So when I saw the email open on his computer, I swear I looked away.

But then my brain said, *Hey, Clara, I'm pretty sure that email said* confidential. *You should check that to make sure,* and, in my weakness, despite the 95 percent probability that I hadn't been raised in a barn, I said out loud, "Yeah, okay."

## THE EMAIL SITTING ON A MISSING MR. CAYWELL'S COMPUTER

Part A: The Email

To: All Faculty, All Staff

From: m.walsh@luptonacademy.edu

Subject: FWD: Confidential—School Policy Updates

To Our Wonderful Faculty and Staff,

The school board has met multiple times over the summer, and we're pleased to announce to staff the following amended changes to school policies and procedures. We request that these changes be kept confidential until the public announcements are approved by the board.

a) Please remind students that no one is allowed past the railroad tracks during class hours unless crossing the Earth Foods greenway with permission to leave school. It's also advised, though the tracks are inactive, not to lie on them or use them for filming a death scene, or, rather, any scene for a student film without permission. Considering our location, it's important that any filming be cleared through the correct channels, including our neighbors, so that they do not think an actual murder is taking place.

b) The hours for the SnackBox have changed in an attempt to ease campus congestion during games. You can now order food starting a half hour before game start time. Go Volcanoes!

c) Lupton Academy is a private school built on core principles we've believed since our founding: Focus. Knowledge. Impact. Focus leads to knowledge and knowledge leads to impact, in our students and, ultimately, in the world. To support our core principles, we're expanding our list of prohibited media. The consequences for bringing such media or discussing it on school property

follow our current disciplinary framework: three strikes to
suspension.

Part B: My Subsequent Reaction

### B.1: THOUGHTS

"Prohibited media"? It sounded somewhat innocuous,
but something pulled at my gut, telling me that it was
policy-ese. Synonyms for *prohibited* included *banned*. Synonyms for *media* included *books*, *videos*, *board games*, and
*games*, and considering that LA didn't seem like it'd wage
war on Uno, nor did its students spend *any* time watching
TV at school, then what was left?

Digging myself deeper into a privacy-invading hole, I
opened the PDF attached to the email and was met with a
list of over fifty "prohibited" books.

*The Catcher in the Rye* for "unsuitable language."

*Beloved* for "exuberant violence, sexual material, and
language."

*Flowers for Algernon* for "offensive representation of a
mentally disabled character."

And the masterpiece.

The finishing touch.

*Don't Tread on Me* for "divisive content, homosexuality," and some other legalistic ass-covering BS that didn't make a lick of sense.

"Go jump off the Market Street Bridge, Lupton Academy."

## B.2: OTHER THOUGHTS

WTFWTFWTFWTFWTFWTFWTFWTFWTFWTF
WTFWTFWTFWTFWTFWTFWTFWTFWTFWTF
WTFWTFWTFWTFWTFWTFWTFWTFWTFWTF
WTFWTFWTFWTFWTFWTFWTFWTFWTFWTF
WTFWTFWTFWTFWTWTFWTFWTFWTFWTF
WTFWTFWTFWTFWTFWTFWTFWTFWTFWTF
WTFWTFWTFWTFWTFWTFWTFWTFWTFWTF
WTFWTFWTFWTFWTFWTFWTFWTFWTWTF
WTFWTFWTFWTFWTFWTFWTFWTFWTFWTF
WTFWTFWTFWTFWTFWTFWTFWTFWTFWTF
WTFWTFWTFWTFWTFWTFWTFWTFWTFWTF
WTFWTFWTFWTFWTFWTFWTFWTFWTFWTF
WTFWTFWTFWTFWTFWTFWTFWTFWTFWTF
WTFWTFWTFWTFWTFWTFWTFWTFWTFWTF
WTFWTFWTFWTFWTFWTFWTFWTFWTFWTF
WTFWTFWTFWTFWTFWTFWTFWTFWTFWTF

WTFWTFWTFWTFWTFWTFWTFWTFWTFWTF

WTFWTFWTFWTFWTFWTFWTFWTFWTFWTF

WTFWTFWTFWTFWTFWTFWTFWTFWTFWTF

WTFWTFWTFWTFWTFWTFWTFWTFWTFWTF

WTFWTFWTFWTFWTFWTFWTFWTFWTFWTF

WTFWTFWTFWTFWTFWTFWTFWTFWTFWTF

WTFWTFWTFWTFWTFWTFWTFWTFWTFWTF

WTFWTFWTFWTFWTFWTFWTFWTFWTFWTF

WTFWTFWTFWTFWTFWTFWTFWTFWTFWTF

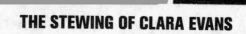

## THE STEWING OF CLARA EVANS

*It may be unfair, but what happens in a few days, sometimes even a single day, can change the course of a whole lifetime. . . .*

—Khaled Hosseini, *The Kite Runner*

"What?" I said to the screen, then promptly stared at it for what seemed like hours, even though it was impossible for it to actually have been that long, because I hadn't heard the bell ring. Or maybe I hadn't heard the bell ring because I was so mad. Not only that, but I wasn't even supposed to know, so I couldn't even talk about it with anyone. I'd have to die bitter and alone, holding on to the secret that ruined my senior year.

"What's up, Clara? Long time no see. How was your

summer?" a voice said. I looked up. It was Mr. Caywell.
Typically, that was when a normal human would say, *Hi,
yeah, for real, I haven't seen you in so long,* and then ask
about the other person's summer, but because I'd apparently been raised in a barn, I didn't. I just looked at him
with my mouth hanging open.

After a long stretch of silence without getting an
answer, he answered for me. "'It was good, Mr. Caywell. I
had a great time and don't want it to end.' Ha. Well, you're
a senior now, so you've only got to deal with Lupton one
last time." He switched back to a fake-me voice. "'But I'll
miss it so much. You've changed my life, and I'm going to
go make millions of dollars because of the education you've
given me and then make an anonymous gift to the school,
simply so you can have an untouched acquisitions budget
for the rest of your tenure here.'"

I said nothing.

He frowned, then looked at me standing behind the
desk, and then cursed. "You read the email."

I nodded.

"Clara."

"I know. I know. Don't read other people's emails."

He stormed behind the desk and minimized the browser window, as if doing so could make me unsee it. "You can't tell anyone about this. If you do, I'll get in serious trouble. You're not supposed to know this."

"Were you going to keep the juicy tidbit that the school is planning to ban fifty books all to yourself? 'Hey, Clara, pull these fifty books off the shelf, please.'"

"Calm down, and, yeah, that's what I was going to do. Are you staff? No. You're not."

"I'm more staff than that adjunct teacher Walden What's-his-face."

He held up a finger to object, but then nodded.

"What do we do?" I asked. "This is like . . . exactly what they did when they tried to ban *The Hunger Games*."

"*Tried* to ban?" he asked. "They *did* ban *The Hunger Games*. And *The Adventures of Huckleberry Finn*. And *The Color Purple*, but those two were before your time." He looked around, checking to see if anyone was listening. "I'm pushing back on it. Fifty is ridiculous. That's why I wasn't here when you intruded on my inbox. I was looking for Dr. Walsh."

"Did you find him?"

He nodded. "Barely."

"And?"

"And I'm not going to give you any more details. You're not even supposed to know this is happening."

"Mr. Caywell. Come on. Who fixed the computer-bar outlet problem?"

He didn't answer.

"Who got Greentree Furniture to donate the library shelves?"

He rolled his eyes, grabbed a bunch of new books off the cart next to the desk, and started putting them onto the shelves. I followed him.

"Who upgraded the cloud storage on the tablets, got the Von Lemetts to donate copies of Photoshop for each computer in the library, and keeps your desk clean?"

"Clara, it's not going to happen. Let it go."

I crossed my arms. "Who was going to organize the processing room this year?"

He looked at me. "You wouldn't not organize the processing room."

"I'm a volunteer. I don't have to do anything."

"You're physically unable to quit this place."

I raised an eyebrow.

He sighed. "Okay, but this does not leave this library. Do you understand?"

I nodded.

"I need you to say it out loud with your words. "'I, Clara Evans, understand that this doesn't leave the library on penalty of being banned from the library.'"

"You wouldn't."

He raised an eyebrow.

"Fine. Fine. I, Clara Evans, understand that this doesn't leave the library."

"'Under penalty.'"

"Whatever—that's understood."

"'Under. Penalty.'"

I sighed. "Under penalty of being banned from the library."

"'In Jesus's name, amen.'"

"In Jesus's name, amen."

"The board and Principal Walsh want me to pull all the banned books from the library."

"Didn't the school want you to pull *The Hunger Games* from the shelves? They're still there, though. Right?"

"All three copies have 'mysteriously' disappeared off the shelves. Actually, if you bring it up in the system, it says we have copies of *The Hunger Games*, *The Color Purple*, and *Huck Finn*, but if you check the shelves, they're all gone."

"Are you serious? I didn't know that. How did I not know that?"

"I don't know. Why would you if you weren't paying attention? You probably thought they were either checked out or lost."

"Why haven't you done anything, Mr. Caywell?"

He laughed. It was a laugh of context. Context I didn't understand. "I've done what I can, but the crux of the matter is we're not a public institution. I'm at the whim of the board and the administration. If I made a huge to-do about it, I'd lose my job. I'd rather be here to point students in alternative directions, or even to point them toward checking the book out at the Chattanooga Library, than not be here at all. Sometimes the game has to be played by someone else's rules. And sometimes those rules don't benefit the players. The thing is, if you don't play the game at all, you can't help others win."

I plopped in his chair, stunned.

Levi.

Joss.

Guy Montag.

Katniss Everdeen.

Clara Evans.

A history of heavy-handed administration. Right under my nose, and I hadn't even known.

## TINY LITTLE LIBRARIES

*A lot of people were afraid of silence, but, in my experience, the silence was where most of my best ideas came from. It was no different standing in front of the cave. No different when I wondered: What if we welded the world back together where no one was looking for a seam? What if we started a library?*

—Lukas Gebhardt, *Don't Tread on Me*

"I'm so mad I could film a murder scene on the train tracks."

"You don't want the neighbors to freak out." He reached under his desk, then put a yellow metal bucket of cookies-and-cream Hershey's Kisses in front of me.

"Are these supposed to make me complicit? How many

more times are they going to pull books? They're pulling *Bridge to Terabithia, East of Eden, Invisible Man,* both of Lukas's books—literally any book that's *about* something is gone. Those are the books that changed my life. How can they pull those? God. They can just do whatever they want. No one cares. *Panem et circenses.*" I grabbed a handful of Kisses anyway, unwrapping three and shoving them all in my mouth.

I looked out the window, catching a glimpse of a row of massive magnolia trees lining the front entrance to the school. The magnolias reminded me of standing outside only twenty minutes ago. Back when I thought I could hear nature symphonies. Now all I could hear was blood rushing through my ears.

"Ugh, I'b so mab."

"Well, take comfort in the fact that I'm not pulling them," he said. "It'll be like all the other times. I silently don't pull them. They silently disappear. I silently put donated copies back into circulation. Those silently disappear."

*Silently.*

*Silence.*

*Where the best ideas come from.*

The thought trickled into my head just like that.

"I've got an idea," I said, grabbing the chair rails. "Let's pull all the books they want to get rid of and I'll keep them safe until something happens."

He frowned. "Or nothing happens, which is more likely the case. You need to realize that."

"Let me do it," I said. "It'll be fine. I'll get them off school campus; no one will know. I'll disperse them into the TLLs."

"The TLLs?"

"Tiny Little Libraries? The things that made me a finalist for the Founders Scholarship? The things that are going to bring me to Vanderbilt?"

"You're a Founders Scholarship finalist? I didn't know that. Wow. Congrats, Clara. That's huge! My sister was a Founders Scholar back in the day."

I smiled for the first time since I'd read the horrid email. "Thank you."

"Wow, that's incredible. We should talk more about that, but, anyway, so you'd take the books and put them in your libraries? How many do you run?"

"Well, the organization runs them."

"The organization?"

"Mr. Caywell, did you not read any of my emails this summer?"

He grimaced.

I frowned. "I started a nonprofit called LitHouse that accepts book donations, runs the TLLs, and also gets high-quality books donated to school libraries in need. We just got a grant from the Offerson Foundation."

"No sh—idding. That's incredible. What kind of super-human are you?"

I shrugged. "I was bored over the summer."

"When I was your age, and I got bored in the summer, I just smoked weed."

"I mean, my choices were between help the city and smoke weed."

Mr. Caywell considered my idea. "If these books are dis-appearing anyway, they might as well go to another place where they'll be used. That's a good idea, Clara. It sucks that we have to do this, but that's the best outcome I can think of. This is awesome."

"Yeah," I said. "I know."

A few seconds of silence ticked by.

"Why?" he asked.

"Why?"

"Why start a book nonprofit? Why not smoke weed?"

"Like I said—"

"No." Mr. Caywell cut me off with an all-knowing smile. "No, that's not it. Give me the real why."

"Well, my parents were—and still are, I guess—airtight budgeters, and because of that, they're terrified of library overdue fines. I loved books; we couldn't afford them. So the deal was I could go to the library to read, but I couldn't check things out. We went to the library a lot. And the library days were some of my favorite memories. The only problem with the deal was, I always wanted to bring the books home."

He nodded. "Books will do that to you. Did you ever sneak one out?"

I faked a gasp. "I would never desecrate the Dewey decimal system with that sort of heresy."

He crossed his arms.

"Yes. Well, for a little while I snuck books from the library by dropping them out the only first-floor window without a screen, which I still feel guilty for. But one day I found a stranger's library card and I used that to check out books. Never got in trouble. And I also want to note that I never once got overdue fines, well, or the person whose card I stole never got fines. Anyway, all this is to say I didn't think it was great for me to have to drop books out windows so I could read, and I didn't want having books in the house to be as hard for other kids as it was for me. So, I . . . started the thing."

"Do you still use that library card?"

"No, I finally got my own card last year and swore on a Bible to my dad that I'd pay for overdue fines if I needed to."

He nodded, then waved toward the stacks. "Then take them. But you better do it quick. Dr. Walsh knows I'm not going to pull them, so I'd bet anything he's already dispatched the order to his minions."

I nodded, opening his email back up and printing out the list.

"Hey!" He said. "Seriously? That's still my private inbox."

"I need a list so I can know what to pull!"

"Well . . . just . . . shred it or something when you're done."

I grabbed the list from the printer and got to work.

"Where are you going to put them for now?" he asked, then said, "Actually, you know what? I don't want to know." He stood up from his chair, and walked out from behind his desk. "I'm going to go to the bathroom and then find Dr. Walsh and tell him we're getting rid of the books. That'll keep him at bay for a bit." He paused; then, louder than necessary, he said, "Whatever you do, don't touch those banned books."

I smiled, and in the same louder-than-necessary tone said, "Yes, Mr. Caywell, sir."

## AND THEN I IMMEDIATELY TOUCH
## THE BANNED BOOKS

I didn't have time to walk several piles of books out to the car, and my locker was closer. It was a dilemma. Did I risk keeping them in the school and sneaking them out later? The answer, of course, was yes. I was no stranger to literary skullduggery. I'd been sneaking books for most of my life, and it had always gone well.

The halls were filled with people now. Classmates doing the normal student thing, getting books and supplies for the day, mostly all the things that were *not* smuggling books about to be banned from the school library. I knew I was running out of time, so I bolted to my locker, which was right around the corner and half a hall down from the library. I opened it for the first time that year and immediately started to stack books inside.

Then, praying that no staff would roll up on me, I ran back to the school library again, pulling more freshly banned books. Luckily, all the time I'd spent in the place guided my hands. Having packed the books away for the renovation and then unpacked and reshelved them box by box, I knew the shelves like I knew the alphabet, letter by letter.

I'd pull about five or six, run to my locker, shove them in, then go get more. I filled my locker up in four trips, then I ran out of room in mine, so I opened my best friend, LiQui's, empty locker, which was only three down from me—she didn't use it—and started filling hers, too. Then, when I was only three-quarters of the way through the list, I suddenly noticed I was the only one in the hall, and, as if telling me that this year was truly going to kill me, the school bell rang.

I groaned and banged my head against the book pile in LiQui's locker.

I sighed, then went back to the library to get the last of the books, wondering if it was even possible for the day to get any worse.

# THE ANSWER

Yes.

Yes, it could.

## FOUR YEARS, FIVE BOOKS,
## FIFTEEN MINUTES LATE

It wasn't a secret I was a very bookish person. I'd been accepted to Lupton Academy, one of the best schools in Chattanooga, with bountiful scholarships, because I wrote a giant application essay paralleling my desire for academic excellence to the appetite of the protagonist in *The Very Hungry Caterpillar* (i.e., the caterpillar) by picture book author/illustrator Eric Carle.

I'd built my entire—albeit relatively short—existence around books. Not because I didn't have friends, but because, since I first learned to read, books had separated my years. Where some people defined their years by grade, I defined mine by the book that had changed me the most that year. So far, in high school?

Freshman year: *Speak*.

Sophomore year: *The Perks of Being a Wallflower*.

Junior year: *The Catcher in the Rye*.

Senior year: Going out on a limb here, but . . . *Don't Tread on Me*.

Each book built me. Each page assembled me piece by piece.

Here's a quick rundown of book ripple effect. I found *A House of Wooden Windows* on a Writers of Color list in the Chattanooga Library my last year of middle school. Reading it made me want to work in a library, so I volunteered when I got to high school. Because I worked in a library, Mr. Caywell recommended *Speak* when I was considering quitting LA because freshman year was filled with bullying and feeling out of place. Because of *Speak*, I stayed at LA and went on a binge of reading all the books known for making people cry. Of course, I found *Perks* quickly after. *Perks* woke me up to the idea that maybe I wasn't the only one who hurt, and maybe every single person had their own cocktail of hurt, just like me, which changed how I thought about the world. I talked to Mr. Caywell about it, and he had this rant that Charlie, the main character from *Perks*, was basically "a chiller version of Holden Caulfield," which obviously brought me to *Catcher in the Rye*. *Catcher in the Rye* combined with *Perks* inspired the idea of LitHouse, and because of it, I was now a Founders Scholarship finalist. One book domino after another.

There was literally no nook or cranny of my life that hadn't been guided by a book, and, for the most part, it had been an uninterrupted journey. No one, especially my parents, had ever told me it was weird, or that books sucked, or that I should really consider what books I put into my brain.

I couldn't understand why LA could overlook all those years. How they could tell me that these books weren't good, or that their content was somehow "inappropriate" for me. Or, if not that, that there was some reason that it was better for me not to read them. That what they had to say wasn't useful or was maybe even harmful. But I was just a kid, right? Just a teen with a tiny brain that couldn't comprehend anything but CW shows, French-kissing, OMGs, and being on my phone.

I never got how the adults at Lupton could tell me, "You're a responsible adult now; you need to act like it.

Come in a uniform. Engage in classes." And then at the same time say, "Actually, you're too young to deal with books about rape, kids being bullied because they're gay, the intricacies of the human condition, and racism." The ridiculous flip-flopping between "you're just a kid" and "you're a grown-up now" depending on the whims of adults was exhausting and infuriating.

It was because I was a bookling that I was incredibly late to my first class of the school year. I ran across school, a method of travel *not* approved by the school board, bolting toward Honors Lit. The class I had dreamed about since freshman year. Good books as education. But I imagined even the class that I'd been looking forward to would be affected by the ban in some way. Maybe all the books I'd learn about were dirty too.

I burst through the door fifteen minutes late. Ms. Lauren Croft (often confused with the tomb-raiding Lara Croft) was discussing her first book choice of the semester, *Their Eyes Were Watching God*, by Zora Neale Hurston. A book that, coincidentally, though not surprisingly, was now sitting in my locker.

I'd had Ms. Croft for English freshman year. If a

faculty or staff member at LA did raid tombs, I wouldn't have been surprised if it was her. She was demanding. Fast-paced. Not one of those teachers who taught the first forty minutes of class like they had all the time in the world, but then realized in the last ten minutes of class how far behind they were and did an info sprint that would be the main cause of varicose veins in Chattanooga teens.

She was a pillar of confidence, and it was very intimidating. Outside of that one English class, we'd sent emails back and forth sometimes when she was looking for books in the library stacks, so she knew me. I wasn't a random LA student. I'd also run into her before at Bookies, the local bookstore, grading papers and drinking a dirty chai latte.

When she turned to see what hooligan was coming through the door fifteen minutes late, the look she gave made me feel like I hated literature and I should drop any sense of book camaraderie we had.

"Sorry," I said out loud, looking for an empty chair. As luck would have it, the only one open was the one right next to Ashton Bricks and Jack Lodenhauer. Both of them were Founders Kids. By *Founders Kids*, I mean great-grandkids of various historical Chattanooga magnates, whose ever-reaching family trees never ceased to show up in the most important places of Chattanooga. These were the kids I'd hated since day one of Lupton Academy.

The Founders Kids (lovingly referred to as F**Ks in text messages with Qui, or as "star-stars" in conversation because "F-star-star-Ks" was a lot to say) were not warm people to be around. They had this smug, puffy aloofness, a sign that no one but those they deemed acceptable was worthy of their words. With the F**Ks, if you weren't chosen—i.e., if you weren't from a Chattanooga power family or generally drowning in money—their hellos weren't greetings, but charity. Their attention wasn't offered; it was given, with the attitude that it was a net loss. A useless transaction that gained them nothing, but lost them the precious time it took to acknowledge that you were there. The fact that they could pay Lupton tuition with pocket change and afford books? Ugh. It made me so mad. Mad that despite my financial aid, my parents still had to stretch to send me there.

There were Ashton and Jack (the former doodling boobs

all over a cafeteria napkin), feeling no pressure to make their private-school tuition money go far. They could go home with a few Cs and it wouldn't cost them anything. They could get a job anywhere with all their connections. If I went home with a few Cs, it'd cost my parents' last three years of hard work and the shot at scholarships at my choice colleges. My parents hadn't been on vacation since I'd started at Lupton. Jack's parents were at the beach every other weekend. The unfairness of it all pissed me off every time I saw them.

I sat down in a flustered huff, attempting—but failing—to not be distracting as I pulled a pen and a notebook out of my backpack. But the pen got caught on the zipper, and it dropped to the bottom of my backpack so I had to fish it out of the pit of darkness. Then, when I grabbed my notebook, the metal binding got caught on the cloth around the zipper and wouldn't come out. Every pull I made unraveled the metal coil, turning my notebook into note pages, which were suddenly flying all over the floor like a blizzard.

Ashton turned to me, raised his eyebrows, then mouthed, *What is happening over here?*

I waved him off and started taking notes on a napkin I found in my pocket until he held out a piece of paper from the floor pile that used to be my notebook. I looked at it, then at him. I didn't want to take it. I really didn't, but I did.

That was it.

I called it then.

Senior year was going to suck.

## FACE-TO-FACE WITH A SLAYER OF BEARS

*Have you ever tried to get to your feet with a sprained dignity?*

—Madeleine L'Engle, *A Wrinkle in Time*

Ms. Croft started talking, bless her heart, but my mind was drowning in the fog of war. I drifted from thought to thought about the banning and what, if anything, I should do about it. I was mad about the whole thing, but the mad that hung around the most was because I'd just been told that my last four years of life were dirty. Somehow, and I didn't really understand how, it felt like there'd been a switch. Like, before the books were banned, they were meaningful words on innocent pages. But now the meaningful words had dirt on them. Like, since they'd been banned, I should feel guilty for having them as part of my own story.

I was even mad about the pure absurdity of some of their choices, like *Don't Tread on Me*. How could you ban a book about the consequences of banned books and not have any thought like, *Hey, this is super ironic—maybe I should reconsider this*?

It made it worse that they were being sneaky about it. That they'd been doing it for years. I mean, I hadn't even noticed that the library stacks didn't include Alice Walker and Mark Twain, and I was the volunteer librarian. How was I supposed to know the difference between the stacks not having a book because we didn't have it, and the stacks not having a book because it was banned?

I can't say how long I thought about stuff, how long I kept saying, *What do I do?* over and over in my head, or how frustrated I was that the banning made me zone out in a class I'd been looking forward to for three years, but when I zoned back in, Ms. Croft's voice was strained, and the room felt smaller—cramped, uncomfortable.

Suddenly the bell rang, but no one moved. Ms. Croft looked at the clock hanging above the door and rubbed her temples. She grabbed a stack of papers and started handing them out. "This is the first two chapters of *Their Eyes*. Read them and then get me a written summary by Wednesday. Don't even think about using SparkNotes; I have their summary memorized. Clara, can you stay for a second? I'd like to talk to you."

I'd already gathered everything and was about to leave when she asked. It sounded ominous. "Yeah, sure."

Strangely, Ashton gave me a peace sign as he left. Of course, Jack didn't even look at me, which felt more normal than Ashton being all buddy-buddy.

I clutched my books to my chest, as if they'd protect me from her fiery glare, and walked toward Ms. Croft.

Ms. Croft was in her early thirties and had these big tortoiseshell brow-line glasses. Tattoos spilled like water down her right arm and peeked through dress necklines, cardigan Vs, and spaghetti straps. Her bangs often pushed to the side, but the rest of her deep-black chin-length hair was pulled back into a short ponytail that curled in on itself rather than floof straight out. She had her head in the universal *I'm so tired and bothered* pose: elbows on the desk, hands over her eyes. She rubbed her eyes, took a deep breath, then sat up in her chair. "You were late on the first day of class. Is this going to be a thing?"

Bad day: 10

Clara: –8

"No, sorry," I said. "I was caught up with a . . . project when the bell rang. It was my fault; it won't happen again."

"What project? This is the first period of the day. Actually, this is the first period of the entire school year. There are no projects."

"Something library-related. Mr. Caywell can confirm. I swear. I'm rarely late to class. I was late to chemistry once, but it was because I'd spilled chicken-noodle soup on my binder and wanted to get all the noodles untangled from the little metal things. Plus, I didn't want to get chicken all over the beakers."

A few moments of awkward silence passed, and right before I was about to ask if I could leave, Ms. Croft sighed again. "I've taught this class for four years," she said. "As a teacher, I know that's not a very long time, but with every class that's come through that door, there are fewer and fewer interested students. Not to mention students willing to let literature tear them to shreds or speak to them. If something happens to these books I'm pushing, are they going to even care? You didn't even care today, and you have the reputation of liking books. Am I doing something wrong?"

She looked at me, and the whole situation, intimidating teacher asking late student what she was doing wrong, just struck me as funny.

I laughed. "Sorry, this isn't funny."

Ms. Croft smiled. "It kind of is."

"I do care, FYI. Ironically and admittedly, I wasn't paying attention because I was thinking about books the whole time."

I looked at her. I didn't know if she was referencing the ban or not with her "if something happens" line, but I knew she knew because the email had gone out to all staff. Did the banned books bother the staff? If it had been happening for years, then the staff had been complicit for just as long. Even Ms. Croft. I wanted to ask her why she didn't do anything, but she was giving off the vibe that she could skin a bear and make a stylish necklace with its teeth, so I decided to not provoke her.

"Why should people care?" she asked.

"About books?"

"About anything? About life outside of what's required of you? About anything that's not *panem et circenses*?"

My mouth dropped. I knew that usage of Lukas Latin. It had been rattling in my brain all morning.

She beamed at my recognition. "You've read it?"

"Of course I've read it. Lukas is my favorite—" I stopped mid-sentence. I had so much else to say, but the book was banned and, despite her being the Honors Lit bear-hunting teacher, I didn't know if she was for or against the ban. I guessed she was against, but simply discussing the book could be a strike and probably a detention, though the email said nothing about it.

Our eyes locked, staring. Wondering. Sewing together mental volumes of translation and interpretation. Her brows narrowed with some sort of distant recognition.

"Wait," she said, an unmistakable edge to her voice. "You're not supposed to know."

"Know what?" I said.

Way.

Too.

Quickly.

She crossed her arms.

It hadn't even been two hours.

## A COMPLEX LASAGNA

"Well, it was nice talking to you," I said, slowly backing away. "Good luck getting the students to care. I mean . . . not that they don't, but I mean, maybe they don't. At least, I'll do better next time. Because I care. Okay. Bye."

"Clara, hold on—I'm not mad that you know. I just don't understand *how* you know. Especially considering that the information was supposed to be confidential."

I sighed. "Because I was raised in a barn. I found out this morning."

She stared at me, one brow raised.

"I accidentally, but sort of on purpose, read Mr. Caywell's email. You can't tell Mr. Caywell I told you. You can't. I don't want to be banned from the library."

"Banned from the library?"

"Just"—I held up a hand—"don't tell Mr. Caywell you know that I know. It's imperative."

"I won't. Don't worry. Isn't this absolutely ridiculous?" she said, shaking her head. "It was so out of the blue. Communication to staff has never been great, but this is unprofessional. I have half a mind to quit."

"Same," I said. "Except then I'd fail senior year and end up living in a box."

She let out a small pity laugh. "How are you taking it so well?"

"Am I? I'm really mad and confused and I don't know how to handle any of it."

"Your mad is a lot different than my mad."

"Well, you should know, the ban is the reason I was in a far country during class. I couldn't focus. It was frustrating enough learning they'd already banned three books, let alone that they wanted to add fifty more."

Ms. Croft's nose scrunched. "I'm sorry, what do you mean?"

"They already banned *The Hunger Games*, *The Color Purple*, and *The Adventures of Huck Finn*. Apparently, like, years ago."

She said nothing.

"Mr. Caywell refused to pull those from the shelves, but they ended up disappearing from the stacks."

"And it's going to happen again?" she asked.

"I guess," I said. "You really didn't know about the others?" I asked, relieved that she hadn't ignored the earlier banned books. But was that the case for most of the staff? Did they not know?

"No. I didn't."

"So, what should we do?"

A few beats of silence passed.

"Check back with me tomorrow. I need to think."

"Yeah, me too," I said, and, not sure what else to say, I started moving toward the door. "Well, sorry I was late, Ms. Croft. It won't happen again."

"Sure. We're going to fight this, Clara. Together. You're the Levi to my Joss."

I laughed. "Levi and Joss would know what to do."

"They would. They'd collect all those banned books before they disappeared and set up their own library. That's what you should do. You run those Tiny Little Libraries, right? Maybe you should do something like that here. Make a library in the quiet of some storage closet somewhere."

Without much work, the thought wedged itself into my brain. A next-door neighbor to the anger and whatever other feelings that had already moved in. I thought about the books in my locker. I also thought about how I'd already snuck books for most of my life. I was uniquely qualified to be a sneaky book peddler. And I thought about the fact that, suddenly, the teacher who could skin bears was on my side, telling me I should start a library.

## THE ONE WITH THE LIQUI

*The needs of a society determine its ethics.*

—Maya Angelou, *I Know Why the Caged Bird Sings*

My best friend, LiQui Carson, and her student cabinet (a.k.a. StuCab) sat at the normal table, which, every year, was "second star to the right, and straight on till morning." (Translated: to the right of the second skylight, to the right again, and against the wall by a big watercolor canvas of an orange sun rising over Chattanooga's Walnut Street Bridge.) I knew the cabinet. We were friendly, but they were only table friends. Once we left the drab slab of laminate, we were practically strangers passing one another on the sidewalks of New York. LiQui was my real-life friend, my only close friend, really, and, to be honest, my only friend in general, and I sat there because she did.

I wondered how I was going to keep the ban a secret from her. Or if I even needed to. If she smelled even a hint of a secret, it'd be dragged out of me with brute verbal— and blackmail—force. That was the problem with time and friendship. Even though she'd been there for every moment of glory, she'd been there for every moment of dirt. I'd learned that, more often than not, when it came to leverage, dirt was more useful than glory.

There was an off chance it'd be a day where she was wrapped up in politics and the student cabinet was a host unto themselves, a conversational train that zoomed along on pure academia and the comparing-penis-size-like act of who could quote the biggest sections of the student handbook. On those days, secrets stayed safe. I prayed to the god of Mondays it was one of those days. I begged the bad day to give me a break, and, before my butt even hit the chair, I knew I'd been tossed a bone. I sat down right in the middle of a rant from LiQui's VP, Scott Wieberdink (speaking of penis size), about some turf dispute between a high school in Alaska and their town's local butchers' union. There weren't enough tiny candy boxes for all these nerds to fit in.

"Hey! How was the annual highlighter all-nighter?" LiQui asked.

"Clara! How was the mango nectar?" Scott asked. "Did you take my advice and ditch the cans and go carton?"

"I did," I said. "And, Scott, I have to say, surprisingly, it was better."

"Ha! I told you she'd join my side," Scott shouted, pointing at LiQui. "Five dollars. In my hand. Prontos."

"It's *pronto*," LiQui said, reaching into her back pocket for her wallet.

"When speed is of the essence, you say *prontos*. And it is. I need to buy a Pellegrino so I can walk by the star-star table and impress Resi Alistair."

"Dude," LiQui snapped, "you don't have to say her full name. We've talked about this. It's real freaking weird when you only refer to her as Resi Alistair."

"I think he feels fuzzy when he says her full name," I added, actually thankful for the mental distraction from trying to figure out what to do, and how I felt, about the ban.

Scott snatched the five-dollar bill out of LiQui's hand and pointed at all of us as he walked away. "Like a damn peach."

"That boy does not have the income to get Resi to notice him," LiQui added.

"He's got five bucks," I said. "I'd notice a boy with one dollar and a book. In fact, I hav—"

"You think five bucks bought those pants?" LiQui asked, nodding to Resi, who sat at the star-star table. "That knee rip alone cost more than his Pellegrino."

Once, Resi and I had found ourselves sitting next to each other in the library. I dropped my only pencil under her chair and had to sneak around her to get it. I had to squat on all fours like Spider-Man, trying to get the stupid thing back. She didn't offer to help. Didn't move. She didn't even look at me. So it was beyond me why Scott would ever be interested in her.

"Y'all hear about Jack Lodenhauer?" Avi, LiQui's treasurer, asked. "He got pulled over going home from a party the other night. He was as drunk as a skunk, but the cop knew his family and let him go. Pretty sure the news didn't even make it to Principal Walsh."

"I'm not surprised," I said, and there was a reason.

Jack's mom, Mrs. Lodenhauer, was the head of the Lupton Academy Parent Advisory Committee (LAPAC) and the founder of a nonprofit that my nonprofit had considered working with at one point (before I decided the Lodenhauers were junk people): Chattanooga Educators' Commission for Change. Jack's dad's grandfather, Charles Lodenhauer, a Chattanooga railroad industry magnate, had been a founder of LA, and the namesake of LA's Lodenhauer Hall, the building that housed the computer lab. Mrs. Lodenhauer's cousin, Rebecca Hursting, was the head of the Lupton Academy Board, or LAB. LAB shared members with the Offerson Foundation, the foundation that had given LitHouse a grant. LAB also shared two or three members with the Founders Scholarship selection committee. Basically, if you were rich and/or a Lodenhauer you were on a million boards at any given time.

It seemed evident that Jack Lodey, the aforementioned trash can, and his freshman brother, Emerson, were destined for a life of board meetings, and I held no envy for that part of their lives. Jack was also, strangely, a Founders Scholarship finalist. It wasn't normally common knowledge who was chosen as a finalist, but Jack Lodey had been on the front page of the local newspaper, with the headline "Lupton Academy Student Follows in Family Footsteps with Founders Scholarship Recognition."

"He'll probably win the Founders Scholarship," I said. "His mom won. That probably means something. Last year Camille Wimarot won, and she was practically Jack Lodey before Jack was Jack Lodey."

"Wow. I forgot about her. What's she up to now?" LiQui asked.

"Got kicked out of Yale for dealing coke," I said.

"What an exemplary show of student leadership."

Scott walked by Resi, cracking open his Pellegrino. Resi looked up. It was quick. A small habitual glance, more in reaction to a new noise than from curiosity.

I don't know if it was because thoughts of the ban had been pushed aside by discussions of the star-stars, but I had an idea. "LiQui, do you mind if I talk to you about something later?"

"Always. Well. Unless it's about the Mav. I'm done talking about the Mav."

"It's not about the Mav."

"Ugh, the Mav," Avi said.

Suddenly, even though no one wanted to be thinking about the Mav—LiQui's ex—everyone was thinking about the Mav. Well, everyone except me. I thought about the ban. And how horrible the day had been, for reasons I couldn't even put into words yet. I couldn't shush the Ms. Croft voice in my head as she told me over and over to make my own library.

It wasn't lost on me that I had a locker full of books.

And it definitely wasn't lost on me how easy it would be to start one.

## FRIENDS IN HIGH PLACES

After school, despite just wanting to go home, I wandered around the administrative wing of Lupton Academy. LiQui had told me that the student-cabinet office was over there somewhere, but it was as unfamiliar as a Bed Bath & Beyond. Despite being best friends with the student-body president, I'd never gone to her office. Why would I have needed to? Anything that made me mad at LA I immediately forgot about when I went home for the day. The StuCab was her realm. The library was mine. That was why, five minutes into my search, I'd only seen the administrative offices and a fancy low-calorie-snack vending machine I hadn't known Lupton had.

My idea was to discuss the prior banned books—*The*

*Hunger Games, The Color Purple*, and *Huck Finn*—not the current ban. I thought that, maybe, if I started in a place that was already "general knowledge," so to speak, then I could push back on the bigger ban I "didn't" know about with the smaller ban I "did." I thought that, maybe, if I could get the student-body president to sign off on some sort of grievance letter, that'd be all the school needed to start a discussion around books and why the administration felt that my life had been a pile of dirt up until that point. And maybe, why they felt some books were more beneficial *not* read by their students?

The student-cabinet office didn't have a nameplate on the door, and it was between two other offices, so I ended up walking by it three times before I got frustrated and started peeking into rooms. Finally I saw LiQui sitting at a desk behind an oval conference table.

"Hey, corrupt politician. Where are your minions?"

"Who knows. Probably gone already. It's all right. I don't mind being left with the mess. It gives me an excuse to not go home."

"So inglorious."

"It's good. Seriously. I'm not in it for the fame; I'm in

it for the change. Anyway, we're not talking about me. What's up?"

I told her about the books that had been quietly banned. My plan of writing a letter endorsed by the student-body president.

And I very, very carefully left the current ban out.

"So you're telling me we used to have these books and now we don't?"

I nodded.

"I mean, yeah. I'll sign that. That's ridiculous. How long has it been going on?"

"Years, apparently."

She pulled out a pen and a piece of paper. "The process when it comes to complaints about leadership: you give them to me, and if I can't solve them, then I sign off on them and give them to Principal Walsh. Who should respond, when he's not busy waging wars against beef propaganda."

"I'm sorry, what?" I asked.

"You read that article in the *LA Bottler* today about how students could help the cafeteria workers keep the cafeteria clean, the one that had nothing to do with how LA food tastes?"

I shook my head.

"Well, according to my sources, Prince Walsh is writing a correction article saying that the newspaper 'painted the staff in a bad light and that the article is wrongfully making people suspicious of our beef.'"

I laughed. "Beef propaganda. He's okay with saying books are useless, but he'll fight to the death for Lupton's beef?"

"I guess. So, let's write this fire right now, while you're here. I'm down for the fight. Why are you mad about it? Let's start there."

"Why am I mad about it?" I asked.

"Yeah, what's driving you to write this letter?"

"I don't know yet. I'm just . . . I'm mad."

"Okay, well, there's not much punch to that. You've gotta turn it up a bit."

"I'm mad that they'd ban books that changed my life, writing them off as dirty. Mad and offended that they think I can't handle them. My whole life has been touched by this list of books. LitHouse. The library. I mean, my whole life. And they're saying it's wrong?"

"There you go." She started writing. "Also, I know you

didn't tell me all of your plan. Where's the good stuff?"

I sighed. "You mean the part after the school repents their sins? Where Lukas and I make out on a pallet filled with autographed books, and he buys me really expensive watches?"

"Uh, yeah? Do I look like I can't handle that?"

# THE LETTER

~~Dear Dictator~~

~~LA Big Brother~~

~~Jerk of Unusual Size~~

Principal Walsh,

I recently went into the library to check out the book The Color Purple by Alice Walker. To my surprise, our library didn't have it. A lot of people consider this book a classic. Not only that, but an important book for students to read.

I asked the librarian if he'd accept a donation of a copy, and he said, "No. It would disappear." I pushed for more clarification and he mentioned that the book *was banned along with a few others, years ago.*

*As of right now, all I'd like to hear is an explanation as to why your chosen course of action for these books was to ban them. I'm simply at a loss as to how this fits under the three principles of Lupton Academy.*

*I hope this discussion will lead to a greater discussion, and, possibly, a better solution that can be approved by leadership.*

*Sincerely,*

*Clara Evans,*

*with approval from LiQuiana Carson, student-body president*

## A LACK OF COPING SKILLS

As I drove home, I thought about the day. From its crappy start with my having been raised in a barn, to Ms. Croft, to the sad fate of being next to Ashton Bricks in Honors Lit. Everything churned like an unfortunate-event stew in my gut. There was no one I could talk to about it, so all the steam was trapped inside. Even the queso in my future couldn't ease all the feelings. I couldn't figure out why, or even how, someone could say that a story was inappropriate to read. Had I missed something? Was I the butt of some joke? Were books the spinach between my teeth no one had told me about, and I was just walking around smiling at everyone?

When I got home, I stormed inside our house, slammed

the door behind me, and walked straight to the fridge. I needed to curb the bitterness quick, so I ripped the door open, causing all the sauce, dressing, and condiment bottles to rattle against one another. I grabbed barbecue sauce, bacon bits, and a block of cheddar cheese. I set them on the counter and fished a plate and a bag of baked potato chips out of the cupboards.

And then I made some damn vittles.

Because I was mad.

Mom appeared from the living room as I was shredding half the cheese block. "Welcome home, honey. Oh, what are you doing? Whoa, easy. I need some cheese for dinner tonight and I don't have a coupon for another bag."

She always spoke with this poetic cadence. She had the kind of vocal tone you could get lost in if she was telling you some story from her day. Dad always told her she needed to start a podcast, but her graceful voice did nothing for me.

I put the cheese in a Ziploc bag, opened the fridge door, and threw the block inside.

"Uh-oh," Mom said, "you're making aggressive vittles. What happened?"

I held up a hand. "I don't even know yet. I'm just mad."

I threw the plate of potato chips covered in cheese and bacon into the microwave and punched in 01:00.

Mom sat down at the kitchen island. "You want to talk about it? I just got feedback on the thirtieth version of a logo for a client and I don't want to see what they said. I'm all ears."

I shoved my hand into the potato-chip bag, breaking a few on the way in. "That's the thing. I don't know what to even talk about yet. It's complicated. Sorry. I'm not trying to be vague. It's all too fresh."

"I understand," she said, grabbing a chip out of the bag. "You're just like your dad. You can't talk about it until you've parsed every bit of it to death." She shook her head. "I'm stuck in a house filled with internal processors."

I grunted and pulled my vittles out of the microwave. The sight of bubbling cheese was comforting.

Mom stood. "Well, when you figure it out, you'll tell me, right?"

I sighed. "Yeah. Heads-up: I won't be around for dinner. Book club night."

"Oh yeah. Well, more leftovers, then. I won't have to

get as much lunch stuff at the store tomorrow." She pulled out her phone and struck something off her grocery list. "Hey, maybe we can go get coffee this weekend and talk? I have a—"

"A coupon?" I interrupted.

She smiled. "Of course. Buy-one-get-one for honey lattes at Good Cup. Maybe we get them to go and take a stroll on the Riverwalk?"

"Okay." I hugged her. I'd learned at an early age that when Mom offered the use of a coupon, you took it.

After she walked out of the kitchen, I scarfed down the vittles, then intensely considered making more, only talking myself out of it because I needed to go and eat a different cheese somewhere else. I grabbed my copy of *Don't Tread on Me*, got back into my blue and busted Honda Civic, and headed toward downtown Chattanooga.

## QUESO . . . WHAT ARE WE READING NEXT?

When I'd first gone to Mojo Burrito, I hadn't really been too crazy about it, but then they moved to a bigger location and got a bigger kitchen and . . . holy guacamole on a shrimp po-boy burrito. Suddenly it called to me daily. It called to me like the sea called Moana. And the queso? The only thing stopping me from putting that junk in a thermos and carrying it around with me was . . . Actually, that was a good idea.

Anyway, the point was: Mojo was like the Force. You could be anywhere at any time and always sense its presence. If someone used a word containing the letters *M*, *O*, or *J*, oftentimes it was only a matter of seconds before you had a burrito in your hand.

From the first day of Queso, there was always queso. Hence Queso . . . What Are We Reading Next? I prayed and prayed and prayed that the divine godlike substance would make me forget about everything. A sort of strange amnesia queso to put my mind at ease.

A group was already there as I walked up to the table. I slid into the booth side without a single glance to see who'd shown up. There was a rotating cast of about five to ten people. Mostly kids who volunteered at LitHouse or helped run the TLLs. Strangely, mostly kids from other schools (Sean from Hill City Prep, Brittney from Chatt Valley High) who'd found me through the Facebook group I'd started back when I was a freshman at LA and needed a group of people who cared about books.

I dug *Don't Tread on Me* out of my backpack, put it on the table, and when I looked up, Jack Lodenhauer and Ashton Bricks were staring at me. Why were they there? How could they be there? They didn't do stuff like this. Were they just there to make fun of us?

Those questions, and the simple fact that Jack Loden-hauer and I were sitting at the same table, derailed me enough that I stared at him until fellow Quesoian Sean kicked my shin under the table.

I snapped to, the smell of queso bringing me back to earth. And then I panicked. "Right. So. Hey, everyone. I . . . uh. Sorry. I've had a strange day and it doesn't seem to be stopping. I mean, not that, like, y'all are strange. Just that there have been things that . . . that, um. Things that were. Uh. Strange? Okay. I'm just going to start. I'm starting. Gosh. This book." I felt strange that a Lodenhauer was listening to me talk about a banned book even though I knew he didn't know about the ban.

Or did he?

He was a Lodenhauer. They were everywhere. Always listening. Jack was no different. There was very little he didn't know, and that thought threw me into even more of a fluster of flusters. An uncharted sudden hot flash of a panic.

Right when enough silence had gone by for me to have started talking, my phone rang. I pulled it off the table. It was LiQui.

I lifted it up, thankful for the chance to regroup. "Hold on, gotta take this."

I jumped out of the booth and went to the outside patio.

"Hey, thanks for saving me."

"Don't thank me yet," she said. "I've got some crap news."

"Okay?"

"I brought the letter to Principal Walsh right after you left, and dude hunted me down before I could even leave. Last time he moved that fast was when I wrote a prank letter telling him that Mr. Adelwise let the Mav do push-ups during class time."

"Again, okay?"

"He didn't seem frustrated, but it's Prince Walsh. Dude has one mood: congenially forceful. He told me, 'It'd be prudent to simply file the complaints about prohibited media until the end of the year when they can be reviewed by the board.' I've literally never heard of a Lupton policy like that. Something funky is going on, and it has nothing to do with LA's beef."

"Wow," I said. "So, he didn't even mention talking with me?"

"Nope."

"So he's going to ignore me? He's going to tell me every-thing I've believed in is worthless and inappropriate and then not give me a reason for it? Now what?"

"Now . . . I don't know. I'm sorry. It sucks, but this is proof that, as much as they say it's not, the StuCab is made to serve the admin, not the students."

"LiQui, this is getting worse and worse."

"Yeah. Times one hundred. We followed the grievance process. He's the ultimate word on it. It's a private school. You know what? I'm going to dig. I'm gonna dig into this. See if there's something we can do based on bylaws or something."

"Okay."

"Don't give up. Maybe there's another way. Okay?"

"Okay. Thanks, Qui."

I hung up the phone, then walked back to the table. Between Jack and Ashton and the fact that I'd just been litblocked by Lupton, I had a hard time finding the words to start the club off. So much for regrouping. I flipped open my copy of *DTOM*.

"So," I sighed. "How many of y'all were able to read the first few chapters?"

Everyone but Jack and Ashton raised their hands.

"All right, no problem . . . guys," I said, pointing at the

two delinquents. "So, how this typically works is we read the book in advance and then discuss its merits. If it's good. If it's trash. We always try to have something we liked about it, even if we all hated it. Make sense?"

Jack didn't say anything, but Ashton nodded. "Awesome."

"So the book we're talking about tonight is *Don't Tread on Me*, my favorite author's newest book. Does anyone have any thoughts or things we need to immediately go at?"

Sean dove into it, leading us into a discussion around the theme of *panem et circenses*, what Lukas was trying to say with the phrase, and how it showed up, differently, in every character. Levi in that he completely revolted against any sort of entertainment. Joss in that he knew there was importance in taking it easy and not just tossing things out because they brought some sort of pleasure, but how he took it too far.

The whole time, Jack whispered comments under his breath to Ashton, who laughed at all of them. I couldn't figure out if Ashton's laughing was out of habit or because he actually thought Jack was funny. Either way, after the millionth snicker and chortle, the pressure cooker of the day finally pushed me over the edge.

"Okay, why are you here?" I asked them. "Like, if all you're doing is mocking the conversation. What's the point of being here?"

Jack laughed, but Ashton looked wide-eyed and caught. "We weren't—I mean we—we're here to . . . ," Ashton said.

I looked at Jack, expectant. His face went tight and sour. He stood up. "Whatever. Y'all think you're so smart, when all you're doing is farting into air."

A few of the Quesoians started to object, but I held up a hand. "Then you should feel right at home here."

"Jack, dude. Come on," Ashton said. "We need—"

"Let's get out of here, man. We don't need this. This isn't what I thought it'd be. Besides, everyone else is chilling at Resi's pool house. Let's just go."

Ashton looked at me, and I was pretty sure I saw an obvious *I'm sorry* in his eyes, but all he did was stand up and follow Jack out the door. I watched them as they left, wondering what on earth Jack had meant by "this isn't what I thought it'd be." What had Jack thought it'd be? How did Jack even know about Queso?

"Well . . . ," Sean said. "That was badass, Clara."

I took a breath. "Don't mess with Levi and Joss. This book rocked me. Now . . . where were we?"

"Brittney was talking about Lukas's ideas of what it looks like to not live as circus trash."

We laughed.

"Circus trash?" I asked. "Exact words?"

"I mean"—Sean shrugged—"something like that."

"All right . . . well, let's pick back up there, seeing how I just took out the circus trash. Also, before I forget, remember, for next Queso we picked one of my faves, *Perks of Being a Wallflower*."

A round of emphatic yeses echoed from the table, but I was too distracted by an overwhelming bit of righteous bitterness. I was so over the star-stars. One more year and I'd never have to see any of them again.

## MR. WALSH

*TEN MORE LIES THEY TELL YOU IN HIGH SCHOOL*

*1. You will use algebra in your adult lives.*

*2. Driving to school is a privilege that can be taken away.*

. . . . . . . . . . . . . . . . . . . . . . . . . . . . . . . .

*10. We want to hear what you have to say.*

—Laurie Halse Anderson, *Speak*

I dropped my toast on the floor. I brushed my teeth with the wrong toothbrush. It was one of those hot-mess mornings that turned into a hot-mess day as soon as I got to school. I was mad at LA. At Principal Walsh. At the star-stars. All of it. I felt it roiling around me. Heat rolling down my back. A fire sparking in my toes.

I was in front of Principal Walsh's office, walking toward the library to get started on organizing the processing room, when the door that led to all the administrative offices opened. The man I wanted to see least at that moment walked out the door.

"Good morning, Clara Evans," the moth of a man said. "Why are you here so early?"

"Why?" I repeated.

"Yes, why?"

I was uncoffeed. I wasn't awake. And I was still mad at his ridiculous dismissal of my due-process letter. "Why did you just dismiss my letter without even reaching out to me? What's the point of putting processes in place if you're going to ignore them?"

"The letter?" he asked, sincerely confused.

Seriously? He'd already forgotten?

"The letter about the banned books."

"Oh. Ah. Well, I am a busy man and some things, like our stances on prohibited media, are better handled by the student-body president. That's why she's there."

I stared at him.

He smiled. "I can assure you that your thoughts and reasons have been noted, but it would behoove you to remember that you attend a private school focused on giving you the best education possible, and that you should trust the administration to do its job."

"Why did you pull them?" I asked flatly. "Why are these books dirty to you?"

"Dirty? Ms. Evans, I think you're taking this way too personally. Remember our core principles. Focus. Knowledge. Impact. We make our choices based on what we feel supports those the best. I ask that you tread down this path very carefully. You know, to be honest, your tone is very undesirable and not respectful. I'd hate for this issue, for you, to become a burr of shame in the citywide blanket of Lupton Academy pride."

I had a lot of problems with his statement:

- A. What vernacular was he trying to use? Southern post-Victorian?
- B. "Burr of shame in the citywide blanket of Lupton Academy pride"? Not a thing.
- C. What was he even trying to say?

"I understand that, Mr. Walsh—"

"Tut-tut—*Principal* Walsh."

"Principal . . . Walsh, I think books *support* those principles. I know they do. Especially knowledge and impact. When my—"

"This is not open for discussion, Ms. Evans. Now, please, run along. We are both busy and this isn't worth our time."

My mind shot off into a million different directions. All south of happy. None the least bit nice.

"Principal Walsh, you're not listening to me. I am living proof that the books you're getting rid of are—"

"Clara, your responsibility as a student is to abide by the wisdom of leadership and the rules we've outlined in the student handbook, which you agreed to follow upon signing your student contract. This school has the right, and not only that, but the obligation, and the God-given honor, to act as legal guardians for students to ensure their well-being and personal growth, as covered in the constitution, as outlined in the law of *in loco parentis*, otherwise known as 'in place of a parent.' Your argument does not stand here."

I stared at him.

Why did I stare at him?

The ghastly amount of hatred I had for him in that moment. He hadn't even let me finish my argument. How could he know that it didn't stand?

He crossed his arms. Impatient. "What would you like me to do for you, Ms. Evans? You are a student, not an administrator, and I don't think a student can understand the intricacies of policy creation when it comes to the well-being of the greater community. You're mad, I see that, but in my observation, you seem to be taking a non-issue very personally. We feel that certain media is simply not beneficial to our students' growth. It is our right to make that media prohibited, and we are doing what is best. I cannot assuage your anger, nor am I bound to on matters such as this."

I didn't think an asshole with a shriveled dictator mind could understand the simplicity of not being an asshole.

"I don't think that's a fair statement," I said. "I also don't think it's right that you have a bigger interest in beef propaganda than this, Mr. Walsh," I said.

"Principal."

My anger skyrocketed. "I don't agree, Mr. Walsh. I'm sorry."

"Principal Walsh."

"Either way, I don't agree."

"It doesn't matter, and, quite frankly, your attitude on authority is a little sophomoric. Consider this a warning, Ms. Evans. Shape up. Your deviance will only hurt you in the long term."

"My deviance?"

"Ciao, Ms. Evans."

My fists clenched. My teeth pressed into my tongue.

I'd show him how personal this was.

I'd show him I was right.

## SUMMARY OF THE REST OF THE DAY

Bathroom.

Think about what Levi and Joss would do.

Library.

Bring a load of books from locker to car.

Honors Lit.

Remember argument with Mr. Walsh.

Think about sticking it to Mr. Walsh.

Decide not to tell Ms. Croft about the argument.

Think about what Levi and Joss would do.

Load of books to the car.

Bathroom.

Class.

Boiling frustration.

Think about what Levi and Joss would do.

Strongly consider getting ten pounds of food from Earth Foods buffet.

Lunch in cafeteria.

Avoid telling LiQui about my argument with Mr. Walsh.

LiQui makes me cry-laugh retelling a dream about Jack Lodey as a professional golfer.

Load of books to the car.

Class.

Class.

Think about what Levi and Joss would do.

Free period—a.k.a. load of books to the car.

## ON-BRAND

*It's strange because sometimes, I read a book, and I think I am the people in the book.*

—Stephen Chbosky, *The Perks of Being a Wallflower*

When I walked into my house with a massive bag of books hanging off my back, it was so on-brand for me that my mom didn't even notice. With a solid "Hey, Mom!" and a very non-suspicious "Hey, Clara!" back . . .

It was on.

## BLACK-MARKET TACTICS AND BEST PRACTICES

*Before I could argue it, I knew this cave belonged to something. A real library. Nothing forsaken. Nothing tossed aside. Nothing banned. Nothing off-limits. Everything permissible. I'd been claimed as a servant, just as I had to the farm fields, to the gathering of words, regardless if they sat in my stomach well. Plato, Newton, Rowling, L'Engle, Apostle Paul, all in one place.*

*Joss and I were suddenly more than runaway soldiers; we were servants of unity.*

—Lukas Gebhardt, *Don't Tread on Me*

Tactic one: put the aforementioned illegal entity as close to the enemy as possible.

I once heard the story of people growing weed in an

overgrown downtown median a block from the local police department. It was genius, and though I wasn't going to start growing weed in the mulch beds by the school's front doors (didn't want to start a turf war with Jack Lodenhauer), I knew there was a tactic to be learned. Because the police had only found out about said "weed median" when someone told them the story a long time after the operation had shut down. So that was what I did. I found my median and set up shop. Sneaky-book Clara was back in business.

The next morning I showed up at school early, my back seat filled with books that shall not be named. I walked inside—chill, calm—making sure no one was watching me as I unloaded all the backpack's contents into my empty locker. Bringing all the books I'd taken out yesterday back to make my own library. The locker playing stand-in for Levi and Joss's limestone mine. This was what Levi and Joss would've done. What Ms. Croft would've done. What Mr. Walsh deserved. How I'd prove to him that the books he wanted to take away weren't garbage.

I'd devised a whole labeling system, which was important, because I had to disguise book covers. I'd taken every single dust jacket and conspicuous LA library bar code off every book and replaced them with covers made of white construction paper. That way, if someone had one shoved into a backpack with their other books or was, stupidly, carrying one around, neither the cover nor spine would be showing.

Instead of writing the title on the spine, I wrote a letter ID so I could match the ID to the title by looking at a list in an Excel doc on my phone. For example: *The Color Purple*, copy one, was A; copy two was B. *Eleanor and Park* was CC—I had to repeat letters because I had more than twenty-six books.

The real point of the white cover was proof. I wanted to collect quotes from people who read the banned books. Specifically, *A House of Wooden Windows*, *The Catcher in the Rye*, *Speak*, *The Perks of Being a Wallflower*, and an extra, personal copy of *Don't Tread on Me*. I wanted to get as many quotes as I could. It was like a living petition. Instead of signatures, we'd see quotes that showed that these books were as impactful as I knew they were. That they actually mattered, and that I wasn't just a crazy person. Then he'd see. If he could see the amount of change between the pages, he'd change his mind.

On my third trip, I marched through the side doors of the school with the last of the books the same way I had before, but this time Mr. Walsh, my enemy, the jerk of unusual size, walked toward me with his typical rush-toward-who-knew-where fever.

He slowed to make the interception.

"Clara Evans," he said, as congenial as ever. "Why? Why are you so early?"

## HOW TO HANDLE RUN-INS WITH AUTHORITY WHILST MOVING CONTRABAND (TACTIC TWO)

Walk like you don't have contraband.

That's what I kept telling myself when I saw him. Even when he looked right at me.

I wanted to say, *Because you're banning books. Because you didn't listen to a word I said. Because these books aren't just trash.* But, pushing my anger aside, I walked with my head high. I was Joss. I was Levi. I could feel my fake purpose all the way down to my teal-and-purple knockoff Toms—Gregs. However, I wasn't quite sure what to say, and it doesn't matter how purposefully you walk if you can't talk your way out of suspicion.

"Library," I said. "I'm going to the library. I mean, because I volunteer there. I'm going to volunteer at the library. Help Mr. Caywell organize the processing room. That's what we're going to do today, I think. That's all, though. Mostly library stuff."

I realize now I could've just said that first line at the beginning and wiped my hands of the conversation, but panic mixed with *I wanna hit this person with an anvil* made a weak and uncoffeed mind short-circuit.

He smiled and swung his arm like he was about to call me ol' chap and offer to take me hunting with the boys. "Aha! I often enjoy a little early-morning time among the stacks myself. Carry on, Clara Evans, by all means."

He resumed his aforementioned moth pace, and I followed his feverish lead in the opposite direction, amazed at his ability to forget important things.

## WHEN ISSUES ARISE, INVOLVE YOUR FRIENDS WHILST GIVING THEM VAGUE ASSURANCES THAT EVERYTHING WILL BE FINE (TACTIC THREE)

I ran out of room in the lockers. I thought I'd calculated the space perfectly, but I quickly realized that if I wanted to be able to slide books in and out quickly and have a little space to breathe, I wasn't going to have room for everything.

Before, I'd jammed LiQui's and my lockers to the brim, cramming books in without thought to breathing space, but that wouldn't work with a library. I couldn't spend half the time it took to check a book out to someone fighting to get said book out of my locker. I couldn't waste time turning books around to figure out their IDs. It had to be quick. Fast. In and out. So I was stuck. Standing in the middle of a hallway with a sagging backpack. I couldn't bring the load I had on my back back to the car. *I Know Why the Caged Bird Sings* by Maya Angelou, *Animal Farm* by George Orwell, et cetera. They were banned classics.

I'd already filled LiQui's locker, and I had no idea what to do with the excess books. I did know that, at any minute, Mr. Walsh could come around the corner and end everything before it could start.

Ashton Bricks appeared out of nowhere. Thumbs under his backpack straps, he stared at me with this dumb, weird, stupid, annoying smile.

"What?" I said.

"Whatever you're up to—no. I want no part of it." He said it like we'd always been friends. Like we'd been hanging out with each other for all of high school.

"Who says I'm up to something?" I asked.

"You're standing in front of my locker with a sagging backpack looking like you just did LSD."

"Maybe I did."

He gave me a *Really?* look.

I stepped out of his way. He swung his book bag off his shoulders. "Look," he said. "I'm sorry about Jack the other night. I didn't . . . We thought going there would be a good thing."

"He was a class-A ass," I said.

"I know," Ashton snapped. "You don't have to be all snippy with me. I know what he comes off as."

What he came off as? What about what all of them came off as?

"Why are you talking to me?"

He turned on his heel. "Okay. Did I do something to you? You've been like, a nonstop class-B bitch to me since school started."

"School started Monday."

"So?"

"So . . . why do you care?" I asked. "You don't even know me. We've sat next to each other for a grand total of a hundred minutes."

He sighed, then pulled his locker open. Me being the worst person ever, I stared at the wealth of empty space. All he had in there was a rubber ball and a copy of the first season of *The Real Housewives of New Jersey*. LiQui loved that show.

I wanted to groan. Of course Ashton would have an empty locker.

Of course.

Ashton turned back, seeing me staring inappropriately

at his emptiness. He looked at my sagging bag, then back to his locker.

He grabbed the ball and the DVD and shoved them in his backpack. "Here."

"Here?"

He gestured to his locker. "I'll make my pet rubber ball live somewhere else. Besides, last time I saw someone look that thirsty was when Resi thought she could date Jack."

"Thought?"

"Do you want my locker or not? I always put my stuff in Jack's anyway. His is so much closer to everything."

I squinted at him. "What's the catch? You don't even know what I'll do with it."

He laughed. "Clara, you're the most paranoid person I've ever met."

"I'm not paranoid and you haven't met me."

He held out his hand. I looked at it. He closed the gap between our hands and grabbed mine. "I'm Ashton. Nice to meet you, Clara. 'Nice to meet you too, Ashton. You're not what I thought you'd be.'"

I was so confused. I had no idea what to say.

"Well, whatever," he said. "Have my locker. Combo is

621. I'll see you in Honors Lit. Maybe by then you'll have figured out that I'm not trying to take your lunch money."

He turned and left. Locker door open. I watched him walk away. Swaggering like a jock, but different somehow. Like confidence mixed with a lilt that said, *I'm not sure if I'm actually this confident.*

LiQui slapped her hand on the locker next to me. "I know you're not watching Ashton Bricks walk away like he's a whole snack?"

I snapped out of it, then turned around. "What? No. No. No. No. No. Ha. No. Nope."

"More than three nos is a yes."

"No," I said, holding out my hands. "We had this really . . . strange conversation. He and Jack came to Queso Monday night. Plus, the weirdest thing, he's actually trying to talk to me?"

LiQui shrugged. "Oh. People are allowed to do that, you know. Happens all over the world."

"No, I just . . . he's a star-star."

She shrugged. "I know what he is. I'm a politician and *I* talk to you."

"Oh." I waved her off. "You don't count."

"Maybe I should stop talking to you—then we'll see who counts."

"Whose side are you on here, LiQui?"

She held up her hands. "I'm just saying, like, chill out. People can talk to you even if you don't like them. Don't be one of those people who hate people that hate people."

"What does that even mean?"

"Think about it. You're brilliant. You'll get it."

I took a breath, resetting my brain. Calming down. "If you stop talking to me, I'll cut off your tea supply," I say, opening Ashton's locker and stacking more white covers inside. "No more steaming hot cups of Lemon Lifter in the processing room."

"I've been drinking Calming Chamomile anyways. Also, did you say earlier that the bro friends forever were at Queso?"

"Yeah. They didn't stay. I sort've . . . snapped."

LiQui's eyes got wide. "I don't even know how to help you anymore. What's all this junk?" she asked, waving a hand around at the locker.

"A project."

"Clara, what sort of sneak are you sneaking here?"

"Why are you so suspicious of my beef?"

She grabbed the book out of my hands and inspected it. "You're starting an underground library, aren't you?" LiQui asked.

I couldn't help but smile. "No."

She laughed and shook her head. "You've got a big set of ovaries, you know that? Also, 'suspicious of our beef' is for sure going to be what I sign on everyone's yearbook. So check this." She pulled out a giant pile of papers and shook them around. The smirk on her face made me think she'd stayed up all night and found a loophole in the US Constitution.

"Papers?" I asked.

"A bunch of information on contract law." She said it like I was supposed to be as excited as she was about it, but she could just as well have been talking in Old Norse.

"C, you don't know what that is?"

"Qui, does anyone?"

"Yeah. Every ass in this school signed a *contract* that acts as *law*. You're telling me you don't know that?"

I rubbed my temples. "What are you doing with your contract pile?"

"Reading to see if there's any built-in accountability for administration, because there's nothing in our handbook, and faculty and staff contracts are out of the reach of students. But I thought maybe I could infer something by looking through what systems, if any, exist in contract law."

"You're a special one, Qui," I said. "Thanks. I know you're half doing it because you're a robot and love this stuff, but thanks."

She shrugged, then pointed at Ashton's locker. "I'm doing it to help the revo."

I pulled a white cover out of Ashton's locker—*Perks*—and handed it to her.

"Is this the next Queso book?" she asked.

"Maybe. You don't know me."

"Are you shaming me into coming again?"

"I'm just saying Jack and Ashton are coming now. You really have no excuse."

She grabbed it and then shoved it in her backpack. "Nothing like getting your friends to associate reading with guilt."

"It's the only way," I said.

She laughed. "See you at lunch."

My year wasn't starting out well, my feelings were a mess, and I was starting an underworld of banned books. Most things were far from easy, but being friends with LiQui was. I was very aware that she was one of the only things keeping me from being a miserable mess and curling up in a corner and eating a whole pint of thermos queso.

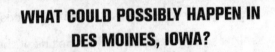

## WHAT COULD POSSIBLY HAPPEN IN DES MOINES, IOWA?

In my first victory of the school year, the lockers were loaded before the bell rang.

I walked into Honors Lit looking smug, cocky, and probably like a vandal, but I didn't care. I felt vindicated. I'd set up my system of proof, and there was nothing Mr. Walsh could do about it.

So there.

I expected something *Their Eyes* related to be on the blackboard, but instead the words *Tinker v. Des Moines* were inscribed in big chalky letters. The lack of *Their Eyes* made sense. It wasn't appropriate anymore. Less valuable than respecting beef.

Ms. Croft sat in her chair and watched students as they

poured into the classroom. She looked over each of us, but when she saw me, she nodded to me with a faint *glad you made it on time* smirk that she'd given me every class since the day I was late. It simultaneously made me laugh and feel like the worst human on the planet. Par for the course with Ms. Croft, it seemed.

Finally, when everyone was there, she stood up from her chair, ventured out from behind the desk, and walked silently straight toward Jack and Ashton. She pointed at a thick white bracelet Ashton had on his wrist that said "Not your forefather's equality."

"That bracelet is for an equal-rights campaign, is it not?"

He nodded, confused as to why she was singling him out in the middle of a class when the most he'd ever gotten was an "Ashton, what do you think the answer is?"

"I'm going to need you to take it off, then. We don't want to protest social issues on school grounds. It's not the place." She held out her hand.

He stared at her, his confusion doubling with each passing second.

"Please, take it off." Her voice went stern. Unforgiving.

On the border of mean and cold.

He took it off, no questions asked, and placed it in her hand.

The entire class could feel something shift in the room as he did, but no one knew what it was. People moved uncomfortably in their seats. Fidgeting away their anxiousness like a pot boiling away water. There was a saltiness in the air that hadn't been there before. An unforeseen grit that rubbed against the backs of our necks. I realized that I was mad, but I again didn't know why. It felt like there'd been a breach of something. A betrayal of time and space.

Ms. Croft felt the unease—I could tell by the way she took slow strides toward the front of the room as if she was giving people time to drill daggers into her back. She placed the bracelet on her desk, right at the front, in the middle, so everyone could see, then turned to face us.

"Good morning!" she said, incredibly chipper. No one returned the greeting. Discontent grew like wildflowers. The air in the room was white static, unmoving but noisy. The silence told a story of opinions being formed, frustrations bubbling up.

She leaned against her desk. "Okay, fine. I'll start. I'm mad. One of the reasons I'm mad is I've been forced to change my entire syllabus for this class. So I thought it'd be a perfect time to go over parts of American history that, I believe, should be necessary to know for anyone who is interested in books. Who knows what *Tinker versus Des Moines* was?"

Again, no one spoke.

"Anyone?"

Silence.

"In 1965, a few students had this idea to wear some black armbands as a nonverbal protest against the Vietnam War. The principal of the school found out and told the kids they'd be suspended if they did. The students wore them anyway. Guess what happened? They were suspended. The parents were upset, rightfully so, and they sued the school for violating the first amendment, the right of free speech. After losing at a district court, and the court of appeals, they took their case to the Supreme Court. All of this took place in a public school, of course. Private schools don't have to abide by public-school rules, but the principle stands everywhere. We are free to protest. There is nothing more American than a protest. The Boston Tea Party in 1773? Protest. The 'I Have a Dream' speech from Martin Luther King in 1963? The Women's Suffrage Parade in 1913? Protest. All of these protests rejected the status quo and had their fair share of naysayers, who called the people who did it ridiculous. It's easy for most to look back in time and praise those who fought for the rights of others. The protests of history are much easier to accept than protests of the present. History doesn't require anything from us. It doesn't even require us to know it. The present? It requires our all."

She looked up at us, then at the bracelet lying on her desk. She picked it up, then walked back to Ashton and held it back out to him. He reached for it, but when his fingers wrapped around it, Ms. Croft wouldn't let go.

"Next time," she said, seriousness punctuating every syllable, "question. Push back. Don't just accept things. Time doesn't change things. Humans change things. Time adapts."

She walked back to the front of the classroom. The class realized what had happened, why she'd taken the bracelet, and how we'd all sat there, complicit. Her point was made.

She leaned against the desk. "Next time, instead of sitting there glaring daggers into my back, do something. Say something. And I don't mean some tirade on a blog or social media that'll get you more likes than solutions. If you don't realize the importance and responsibility of the freedoms we've been given, then you won't realize what freedom actually is." She looked at me as if I needed more persuading. "For the next few classes, we will discuss court cases specifically dealing with censorship and free speech, starting with *Tinker versus Des Moines*. Homework for this, and for the next few court cases we discuss, will be essays outlining the arguments for each side. Am I clear?"

She wasn't happy with the few confused nods she received, so she asked again. "I need to hear you. Am I clear on this?"

A smattering of firm yeses echoed through the room.

I stared at her, more than a little in awe of the way she'd decided to fight Mr. Walsh, and I felt a bloom of pride that I'd followed her advice. That, though I hadn't told her I'd started a library, we were both fighting LA. That I wasn't alone.

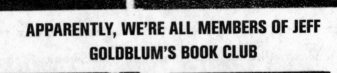

## APPARENTLY, WE'RE ALL MEMBERS OF JEFF GOLDBLUM'S BOOK CLUB

I was putting books back onto the library shelves during my free period when LiQui walked in.

"Hey," I said.

She held up the white cover I'd given to her earlier that day, then pointed at the quietest corner of the library. A spot behind a shelf and in the most non-visible part of the room. A place listed in Forbes Travel Guide's Top Ten Places to Find a Couple Making Out.

I looked back at Mr. Caywell, who was busy typing away on his computer, then followed her into the corner.

"Check this," she said, holding out her phone. I grabbed it and started scrolling. "Prince Walsh sent this to the StuCab after we talked this morning. It's the new student handbook. Guess what's in it?"

"No way," I said. "This is their announcement?"

"More like a bet no one's going to read through sixty pages of updated student policies. You see how they did it?"

The thing was, I didn't see how they did it, which I assumed was the point. "I'm not going to lie, LiQui, I don't know what I'm looking at."

"See? It's doing exactly what they wanted. Look."

I zoomed in on the text, and there was a small section under the rules that said:

*Students should be aware that there are multiple media items prohibited on school grounds, including such books as* The Anarchist Cookbook. *As with all other policy infringements, having these items on the Lupton campus comes with a three-strikes policy. For a complete list of items, please see your student-body president.*

I snorted. "Who's going to say no to that book being prohibited? Especially in the South?" Did they really have the gall to equate *Don't Tread on Me* with *The Anarchist Cookbook*? "That's the most underhanded and veiled insult I've seen at Lupton. Do you even have a list?"

She shook her head. "This is how it works. They're betting their students have too much homework to read for fun. But let's say they do read for fun, and let's say that someone is weird and brings a banned book to school for whatever reason. Well, first of all, have you ever brought a banned book to school? Not recently, but in the past."

I nodded. "Yeah, of course."

She rolled her eyes. "Yeah, well, of course *you* have; you're a bad person to ask. I never have. And that's the reality of it. You're one of the few, Clara."

"Yeah, and you literally just called me weird."

She waved it away. "Anyway, say you bring one of your bannies to school and you get caught. You'll be told 'having your book on campus is against school policy.' If you care enough to ask, 'Well, why?' Prince Walsh will say, 'It's in the student handbook.' But let's say this kid isn't you, and let's say this kid isn't on their A game and doesn't realize that what Prince Walsh said wasn't really an explanation. They say, 'Okay, sure.' They walk away. Prince Walsh doesn't have to deal with it."

"Okay, but what if it *is* me?"

"Right, well, because it's you, and *you're* bringing your A game, you say, 'Well, that didn't really answer my question. Why?' Prince Walsh will say, 'It isn't currently beneficial to your learning environment.' So there you are, the A-game student hearing 'currently beneficial,' thinking the whole situation weird, awkward, and confusing. So you want to get out of the principal's office. You go, 'Yeah, sure,' not realizing you just got censored."

I opened my mouth to push back, but LiQui held up a hand.

"But say you feel weird and driven enough to go through all of that yet still have the energy to read the student handbook. You read what we just read, and then you come to me. I say, 'Sorry, I don't have a list yet. They haven't given me one.' Are you going to go back to Principal Walsh and ask for a list?"

"I mean, right now I would."

"Clara, come on. For real."

I sighed. "Likely not."

"Right. There are all these obstacles that ninety-nine

percent of this school wouldn't cross."

"Why?"

She shrugged. "I don't know. But it's weird, right? It's like it's built this way."

Suddenly, my war against Mr. Walsh felt bigger than it had before.

She held up a white cover. "Well, it can't stop you from doing this. Right? You've gotta do this."

"Yeah," I said. "I'm sick of Mr. Walsh getting away with this. I'm going to show him he's wrong."

"I'm proud as hell. Look, you know books aren't my jam, but bringing power to the people is. StuCab's got resources. You need some extra lockers and unused janitor closets for drop-off places? We got you. I'm doing what I can to find some legal alleys to take this. I've reached out to a few peeps at other schools and emailed the American Library Association."

"Hmm. Well, first of all, I don't understand how anyone can not like reading, but it's fine. We can still be friends. Second of all, maybe. I don't know. It's not going to get crazy enough for me to have to drop them places, I don't think. Besides, I want to be there when I give them out.

Third of all, do you really think you can find something?"

She shrugged. "I'm gonna try. If this was a public school? We'd be all over this. Private schools are different beasts. Law, girl. Sucks."

I laughed. "Thanks, LiQui. Seriously."

She nodded. "Let me know how we can help."

"Well, I have another question."

"Go for it."

"Do you think the administration will notice me? I mean, they're betting that students don't read for fun, right? And if we *do* read for fun, there's a whole library of 'acceptable books.' So, they aren't looking very hard if they think the 'unacceptable books' are gone, which they technically are."

She shrugged. "Hard to notice a tree when you think you're in a desert."

"Right. LA kids aren't lining up to borrow books when they *aren't* banned. So I'm thinking I'll hustle them to the people who are interested. The year ends; we graduate and get out of here. Boom. I've done my part in fighting."

The way I said it sounded so much calmer than the way I felt.

"It's so subtle it'll actually work," LiQui said.

Then, strangely, one of Lupton football's two wide receivers—LiQui's ex, Maverick Belroi—appeared from around the bookshelf, taking my mind off omissions, rejected grievances, and systems of proof. Both LiQui and I stared at him, heads tilted in a *Yo, what are* you *doing here?* look.

What was going on? What sort of parallel universe was sending the people I least expected to the places I least expected to see the people I least expected to see?

I had no idea why he was there, but since he spoke a special language—Let Me Insult Your Deepest Insecurities, but If You Get Mad, You're Insane Because It Was Just a Joke, Bro—I girded myself for some sort of lambasting or insult. LiQui and I both knew this, and her dagger eyes and pressed-together lips were a sign that all her strength was being used to keep the snappy insults at bay.

"'Sup," the Mav said.

"Hi?" I said.

He leaned closer to me, and I began to panic. What if he was attempting to make LiQui jealous by kissing one of her friends? How fast would I perish in the disaster that would follow?

"I heard you're who I should see if I want a copy of a book called *Eleanor and Park* by Rainbow Rowell?"

"Uh . . . yes?"

I had a few more questions for him that went unasked:

*Do you know that* Eleanor and Park *is banned?*

*Are you a spy? Who sent you?*

*How do you get your arms to be that big yet still find shirts that fit?*

Was this really going to be my first book checkout? A banned romance—granted, a brilliant and masterful one—to a jock that an entire school called "the Mav"?

He shrugged and I didn't press any further. I wanted him gone and the moment with LiQui back. Plus, with LiQui looming next to me, I figured the quicker I got the transaction over with, the better.

"I'll be right back," I said to LiQui. Then I silently nodded to the Mav, and in some of the most awkward minutes of my LA career, he silently followed me to my locker.

When I opened the locker to pull out *Eleanor and Park*, the Mav went, "Whoa. Those all books?"

I looked at what was obviously a stack of books.

"No, some are TV dinners in case I don't want what they're serving in the cafeteria."

He nodded. "Sweet. Good idea."

"Yeah, they're all books. All banned."

"LA has banned books?"

I nodded, but I said nothing else. I wasn't lying and I wasn't betraying Mr. Caywell. It had been announced, and according to the student handbook there was supposedly a list of all the banned books with the student-body president. It was public knowledge.

I matched the book code with the ID on my phone and pulled *Eleanor and Park* up from the bottom of the stack and handed it to him.

"Bring it back whole. Oh, and if you could write a quote on the cover, that'd be awesome. Something that you liked about the book. A thought or, like, something that changed you."

The Mav nodded.

I pulled up a personal-library-manager app—yes, they have them—I'd bought for ten dollars on my iPhone. The app let me know which books of mine were borrowed, who had them, what books I hadn't loaned out, and so on.

"Phone number? Address?" I asked. He gave them to me willingly.

"Okay, cool. It's due two weeks from now. You'll get a text in a few seconds with the actual date. Oh, and you'll get a reminder text the day of. If you need to renew it, respond to the reminder text with the word *renew*. If you lose it, you pay for it. If you get caught with it, I didn't give it to you. Okay?"

"So the school banned these?" he asked.

"Yeah," I said.

"Weird."

"Very."

"So this is, like, a stick-it-to-the-man sort of library? Like, a secret library of banned books?"

I nodded.

"Sick."

"Two last questions?"

"Sure."

"Where did you hear about *Eleanor and Park*? And who told you to come to me?"

"Jeff Goldblum was talking about it on his Instagram feed, so I asked Mr. Caywell for it and he told me to find you." The Mav slid the book into his backpack. "I'll bring it back. Peace."

I watched him walk away, then went back to the library to find LiQui swirling in circles on a stool at the computer bar. She stopped as soon as I came in and looked at me with a face I called her *report* face. An eyebrow raised, a slight tilt of her head, lips positioned in such a way that you knew you'd get an earful if you didn't report. But before I could, Mr. Caywell walked up to me with another cart of books. "Here you go," he said. "Oh, did that kid ask you for that book?"

I grabbed the cart from him and pushed it out of the way of the aisle. "Yeah . . . what's that about? He told me you told him to ask me for it?"

He nodded. "You've got more libraries than I do, and those libraries don't operate by the same rules."

"So you're going to send everyone looking for contraband my way?"

"I don't know what you're talking about." He walked away. I realized I'd been given a promise of patrons, and I felt bad that Mr. Caywell thought he was sending them to my Tiny Little Libraries, not a locker library full of banned books. But, out of all the weird feelings I had, that one was one I could live with most.

I walked back over to LiQui with my new cart of books. Her face was still etched with *report, peasant*.

"First," I said pushing a book into the *B*s, "he said he heard about the book from Jeff Goldblum. Isn't he that guy in *Jurassic Park*?"

"Yeah. He's his grandma's favorite actor. She thinks he's hot and made him follow him on Instagram so she can keep up with him. He has a book club, apparently."

"For real?"

"Yep. You have an extra copy of it?" she asked. "I wanna know why it sounded so appealing."

"You should read *Perks* first, but yeah, I've got two. I'll bring one to you."

"What else did Mav do?"

"Well . . . wait. Before we move on, he likes romance?"

She shrugged, jumped off her stool, grabbed a book off the cart, and scanned the shelf for where it went. "Dude is also super obsessed with snapping turtles. Who knows."

As LiQui and I put books back, I gave her the rundown of every step I'd taken with the Mav in tow, with a few embellishments like "I swear he was humming the *Monday Night Football* song as we walked," and even though Mr. Walsh was winning, it felt like a temporary win. Levi and Joss were proof that you could stop a war with a library.

I felt inspired.

I felt strangely hopeful.

## A FANCY LETTER FOR CLARA

*Founders Foundation*

*353 Riverside Street*

*Chattanooga, Tennessee*

*Clara Evans*

*8057 Foundry Hill Drive*

*Chattanooga, Tennessee*

*Dear Founders Scholarship Finalist,*

*Congratulations from all of us at the Founders Foundation on making it to the final round of the prestigious Founders Scholarship. As you know, this is a highly competitive program, and we consider any student finalist the next wave of future leaders in America.*

*Since the foundation's beginnings in 1931, it has been a tradition to host a dinner for the five Founders Scholarship finalists. At this event, you'll be able to meet local leaders and ask them any questions you may have about public work, college, careers, and internships. Then, after dinner, each finalist will have ten minutes to speak to dinner attendees about whatever topic they choose as long as it fits within the themes of community, service, or leadership.*

*You're invited to this event, which will take place on the fourteenth of September at six thirty. Attire is formal. We encourage you to bring two guests.*

*To attend, please RSVP by August 25th by responding to this email. Also, please be sure to list any dietary restrictions or allergies.*

*Sincerely,*

*Shelli Brown*

*Chair of the Founders Foundation*

## A LIST OF POTENTIAL SPEECHES

- ~~Your Letter Makes Me Sound Way Smarter Than I Am~~
- *Don't Tread on Me*: A Community Library
- My Freshman Year as a Library Intern
- ~~The Books That Defined My Years~~
- ~~Why Be a Leader When You Can Sleep?~~
- ~~Please Give Me This Scholarship So I Can Go to College~~
- The Pros and Cons of Private Education
- An Ode to Queso: The Real Community Leader
- LitHouse Stuff?
- ~~Law, Girl. Sucks.~~
- What's the Deal with Books at LA?

132    DAVE CONNIS

- Someone Needs to Make LA Administration Calm Down
- Holding LA Admin to a Higher Standard?
- ~~Our Suspicious Beef~~
- ~~Hey! I'm Running a Banned-Book Library in My Locker!~~
- ~~Hey! I Think the New Book-Ban Policy at Lupton Academy Is Incredibly Dumb!~~
- ~~Hey!~~
- Why Don't We Just Fix All the World's Problems?

## A LIST OF POTENTIAL PEOPLE I COULD BRING AS GUESTS

Absolutely invited:

- Lukas Gebhardt
- Lukas Gebhardt
- Lukas Gebhardt
- Lukas Gebhardt
- Lukas Gebhardt
- Lukas Gebhardt
- Lukas Gebhardt
- Lukas Gebhardt
- Lukas Gebhardt
- Lukas Gebhardt
- Lukas Gebhardt

- Lukas Gebhardt

- Lukas Gebhardt

If that doesn't work out:

- Lukas Gebhardt's hologram

- Levi and Joss

- Dad and/or Mom

## TEXTS FROM THAT NIGHT

Unknown Number #1

**Unknown Number** [6:11 PM] Hey is this Clara Evans?

**Me** [6:11 PM] Sure is.

**Unknown Number** [6:11 PM] This is Resi Alistair. I hear you might have Speak by Laurie Halse Anderson?

**Me** [6:11 PM] Oh, cool. Yeah, that's a bannie, so I have it.

**Unknown Number** [6:11 PM] A bannie? Can I get it from you tomorrow?

**Me** [6:11 PM] Yes. Quick survey, how'd you hear?

**Unknown Number** [6:13 PM] LA library copies were gone for some reason, but the Mav told me you had a bunch of books stashed away.

**Me** [6:13 PM] Ah. Cool. Come by locker 21 before lunch.

**Unknown Number** [6:13 PM] Okay, thank you.


Hanna Chen

**Hanna** [6:55 PM] Hello, Clara. This is Hanna Chen. We were on the track team together freshman year?

**Me** [6:55 PM] Hey, Hanna!

**Hanna** [6:55 PM] Do you have a copy of Strange Astrophysics by Colt Cax?

**Me** [6:55 PM] Uhh. I'm not sure? Let me check. Who told you to check with me?

**Hanna** [6:56 PM] Mr. Caywell. Our library didn't have it, but he said you might.

**Me** [6:56 PM] Sure, give me a sec.

**Hanna** [6:56 PM] Ok. Thanks.

**Me** [6:56 PM] Yep! Meet me at my locker tomorrow during free period?

**Hanna** [6:56 PM] Sure. Thanks.


Unknown Number #2

**Unknown Number** [7:30 PM] Heyyyyy.

**Me** [7:30 PM] Hi! Who is this?

**Unknown Number** [7:30 PM] Ashton Bricks.

**Me** [7:34 PM] Oh, hey.

**Unknown Number** [7:34 PM] Is my locker working out for you?

**Me** [7:34 PM] Yeah. It's peachy. Thanks.

**Unknown Number** [7:34 PM] What are you doing with it?

**Me** [7:34 PM] Just a project thing.

**Unknown Number** [7:34 PM] Cool. Resi tells me you might have a book I need for class?

**Me** [7:34 PM] The Friendly Occultist's Guide to Death Potion Making?

**Unknown Number** [7:34 PM] Ha. Yes, please.

Speak by Laurie Halse Anderson? YA.

**Me** [7:34 PM] Which teacher is still assigning Speak?

**Unknown Number** [7:35 PM] Ms. Croft, English Comp II.

**Me** [7:35 PM] Of course. You have two Ms. Croft classes?

**Unknown Number** [7:35 PM] Yeah, she's intense in both, FYI.

Also, Resi and I were talking about how weird it was that the library doesn't have Speak anymore when I know I saw it on the summer reading list last year.

What's up with that?

**Me** [7:35 PM] Tell me about it.

I have one other copy of Speak.

Want it?

**Unknown Number** [7:35 PM] Yeah. Okay, sweet.

**Me** [7:35 PM] Well . . . you'll need to meet me at your locker.

**Unknown Number** [7:35 PM] Life. Saver. Thanks.

**Unknown Number** [7:40 PM] Wait . . . my locker?

**Me** [7:40 PM] Don't worry about it.

**Unknown Number** [7:40 PM] Do I want to know?

**Me** [7:40 PM] It's fine.

**Unknown Number** [7:40 PM] Right.


LiQui

**Me** [8:22 PM] Yo.

I just had two separate star-stars in my messages asking me for books from my library.

The Mav did some work.

So far Resi and Ashton are the only ones who even find it weird that we're missing books.

**LiQui** [8:22 PM] Things that are worth noticing normally go the most unnoticed.

Cat videos on the other hand? Watch out.

Thoughtful discourse? Nah.

Video of cat accidentally falling behind a couch? LET'S GO.

**Me** [8:22 PM] Freaking panem et circenses.

Seriously how do humans suck that bad?

**LiQui** [8:23 PM] Panem et wtf?

**Me** [8:23 PM] Read Don't Tread on Me.

**LiQui** [8:23 PM] That the one you gave me?

**Me** [8:23 PM] No. It's different. You need to get reading.

**LiQui** [8:23 PM] I just posted a new NOT a cat vid. Check it.

**Me** [8:25 PM] "Call it like it is, crust. Your hair is crust."

I love it.

**LiQui** [8:25 PM] Mojo this weekend?

**Me** [8:25 PM] QUESO QUESO QUESO

## A CRYPTOGRAPHIC BOOKSTORE

Ashton stood at his locker, watching me pull out the *Speak* white cover and begin the checkout process.

He looked around me and scanned the books inside. "Do you know something we don't?"

I looked up. "Why would you think that?"

He motioned to the books. "You've turned my locker into a cryptographic bookstore?"

I turned, glanced at the stacks, then shrugged. "I don't know what you're talking about. You're delusional."

"A joke! Wow. The paranoia continues to abate. What a day. Oh, do you mind if I snag a copy of the next book-club book?"

*"Perks?"*

"Maybe? I saw it on your Facebook group but I can't

remember. I think it had a longer name and something to do with being wallpaper."

I nodded and grabbed a copy of *Perks* out of the locker. "*Perks*. Phone number?"

"Lazy. Grab it from my text last night."

"Can you just give it to me? I don't wanna exit the app."

He gave it to me, and as I typed the numbers in, he said, "You know, it seems to me like you're coming at me with some class-perception problems."

"It sounds to me like you've never wanted to talk to me before and I don't know you very well."

"It sounds to me like we've never sat next to each other in a class before, so talking to you wasn't a natural thing until now."

"It sounds to me like you just like to stick with your own friends."

"It sounds to me like that's what you do in high school and what you really mean by 'friends' is 'income bracket.'"

I didn't have anything to say.

He shook his head, snatched the book out of my hands, and walked away from me again, and, for some reason, that time, I somehow felt like the bigger jerk.

## LOST IN THE WAR

The rest of that day, I did my best to ignore the fact that walking the halls the second day of my library's existence filled me with a thousand pounds more paranoia than the day before. It wasn't supposed to have had that effect, but alas, there I was.

I felt on edge walking between classes, sitting in classes, existing, listening to Ms. Croft finishing her *Tinker v. Des Moines* lecture. Even though she was talking right to my library, I was feeling like, at any moment, I could be busted for pushing good literature out of my locker. I wasn't a sneaky person. The most I'd ever sneaked was a book out a window. Every single Magic Tree House book. I'd felt like an anxious felon doing it and even cried a few times. Now, the pressure pushed at me. I wasn't super sure what I wanted to do for a living, but this was making me realize I'd never make it as a criminal.

I slid through the food line, feeling anxious and short-fused. I proved I was both when one of the lunch workers asked me what I wanted as a side and my immediate reaction was "whatever," and I didn't mean it in the "I'm ambivalent" way.

"You look more miserable," LiQui said as I walked up to our table. "Did you just backtalk sweet Ms. Craig?"

I nodded as I sat. "Probably. I don't even know."

The StuCab minions, Scott and Avi, sat down at the same time.

"How's the book business going?" Scott asked.

"So . . . LiQui told you?"

He nodded.

I'd known word would spread, and I'd wanted it to, but there was something that felt reckless about having people blabbing my secret to everyone. I'd rather it have taken root slowly and silently than with a blaze of flashy fire. I looked at LiQui with a *Hey, do you mind not sharing my illegal library with everyone?* face. She grimaced, a silent apology.

"It's . . . manageable, so far? It's making me paranoid, though."

"The Unlib?" LiQui asked.

"Unlib?" I asked. "Oh," I said. "Underground library. Clever."

LiQui rolled her eyes. "Speaking the full form of the abbreviation defeats the purpose of making one."

"Sorry," I said. "It's hard to keep up when you feel like you're hiding a dead body in your backyard. I don't know, maybe this whole . . . Unlib thing isn't a good idea. I mean, they did it in *Don't Tread on Me*, but that's fiction. Do I dare disturb the universe?"

"What is that from?" LiQui asked. "I know that. What is it?"

"It's T. S. Eliot, but really I'm quoting *The Chocolate War* by Robert Cormier."

"You read that for Queso, right? A long time ago?"

"Yeah."

LiQui nodded. "I loved that book. You know what, maybe I will read that perky book you gave me."

*"Perks. The Perks of Being a Wallflower."*

"Yeah, that. So here's my Q for you: Why are you doing the Unlib?"

I stared at her.

"Hello?" she asked after I didn't answer.

"I think because I was inspired to fight the system by *Don't Tread on Me* and Ms. Croft."

As soon as I said it, I knew it wasn't right—well, at least that it wasn't the whole story.

"So you're doing it because a book told you to?" LiQui asked. "That's not what you said when you wrote that letter."

"I mean, no. There's more to it than that."

"Like what?"

"Like, those books changed my life, and Mr. Walsh shouldn't be able to just ban them, and I want to prove him wrong. They are valuable."

"Why?"

"Because it's wrong."

"Right, but *why* is it wrong?"

"Because these books changed my life."

"So you're running the Unlib because the books he banned changed your life?"

"Yeah."

"Why does that make banning books wrong?"

"Because . . ."

"Well, no wonder you're feeling flimsy about it all," Scott added randomly. "You don't even know why it's wrong.

You're revenge Unlibbing. Power-tripping."

"He's got a point," LiQui said.

I scoffed. I didn't know Scott very well, and there he was telling me I was power-tripping. "So do y'all want me to stop the Unlib until I'm not doing it out of revenge? I already did all the work. People are already checking out books. Besides, if I don't do this, who's going to stand up to Mr. Walsh? No one."

"Chill," LiQui said. "No one's attacking you. Y'all, did you see my new video?" I shot LiQui a *thank you for changing the subject* glance.

I looked across the cafeteria and saw Ashton sitting at the star-star table. And for the first time, I wondered if I was pinning him all wrong, and if I'd been doing it since freshman year. Had I been wrong about what I'd thought was so right? Was I just another person who hated people?

Suddenly I was worried about having gotten Ashton completely wrong, because I felt like if I could be that person, the kind of person who hated without noticing, then I could be wrong about anything.

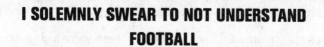

## I SOLEMNLY SWEAR TO NOT UNDERSTAND
## FOOTBALL

*There is nothing that will add depth to despair like the feeling of
deserving it.*

—David Levithan, *Two Boys Kissing*

Cocky swagger boys. Lights. Thick pads. Grunting. Not my
idea of an invigorating night out, but games were games
and support was support.

Lupton Academy loved football. The academic year
seemed to orbit around the Lupton Vols, and, even if you
didn't like football, you showed up at the games because
it was what you did. I sat with LiQui on the bleachers.
Typically, I either brought a book to read or used the time
to answer LitHouse emails, getting donations picked up,

sorted, and brought to where they needed to go. I initially did all the LitHouse stuff myself, but I eventually partnered with a local juvenile rehab program that brought their participants into the mix, trading their work for any book they wanted. I loved knowing there were kids getting fresh air and fresh words and, also, giving me free time again.

Now, at the start of senior year, I was simply pointing fingers, telling people where to go, and shaking the hands of new connections.

"We're looking undeniably like a picnic," I said, taking a break from emails and tucking the blanket under my legs. "Is the Mav still the . . . chase receiver?"

"Not a position," LiQui said.

"What is he, then?" I asked.

"Wide receiver," LiQui added.

"So he catches the ball?"

"No, he runs in place to keep the field warm so others don't get stuck in the grass."

"Oh," I said. "I didn't know you had to do that."

"You don't, C. You don't need to keep the field warm. Were you raised in a barn?"

I nodded. Accepting it. "Yes."

I might not have had physical evidence, but there was enough mental evidence leading me to believe I'd been born in a hayloft and raised by chickens who read people's emails and didn't understand the football, the official language of the South. Some people will tell you it's English. Don't buy it.

"What does it mean when the ref does that squirrelly thing with his hands?" I asked.

LiQui laughed. "You make paying attention impossible."

"Oh, I'm sorry," I said. "Would you like me to suddenly be entertained by football after three years of not being entertained by football?"

"It's not a lot to ask," LiQui said. "I started the application to Vandy last night."

"Qui! The plan is in motion! Yes!"

There were very few things that were set in stone in my life. When LiQui and I met in elementary school, our friendship became one of them, and the two of us going to Vanderbilt University together was the other. These things were nonnegotiable. The problem was, neither of us could really afford to go to Vanderbilt, so we'd both decided to make our own way. Luckily for LiQui, her grandparents had stepped in and paid her way to come to Lupton and also promised to pay for her to go to Vanderbilt—with some stipulations. Luckily for me, I was a massive nerd and did some (apparently) cool things with books, and that had scored me a place as a Founders Scholarship finalist.

"How's the grandparent problem?" I asked.

"Permanent. Gramps is still preaching, 'You go to Vanderbilt and get that business degree. You do good for yourself. Then you can do the same thing I'm doing for you for your grandkids.' Hard to say no when they've footed the bill for all your education."

"Wasn't a business degree what you wanted?"

She laughed. "I'm seventeen. So far the things I've wanted to be have ranged from spaceship designer to YouTube star. I don't know what I want. I mean, a business degree sounded good because it meant an actual job with a promise of cash in contrast to the other degrees. I've just been wondering . . . what if there's something else I want to do? I've never asked because I've always been told what is what."

"Well, is there something else?" I asked.

She shrugged, and the silence that followed was a sign that the convo was done. We watched the Mav make a catch, juke the outside linebacker (yes? That's a thing, right?), and then make a sixty-yard run for a touch-point goal. The obligatory teammate-pile-on-the-guy-who-scored unraveled quickly when the coach started screaming, hulk-stomping his way over to the writhing victory amoeba.

"Wait," I said, "did we not just score?"

"Nah, we did. Coach Camper is always mad about something someone did wrong."

Her voice was tight. Curt. I wasn't sure what I'd said, and I had to pee. So I stood.

"I'll be right back."

"Stay away from the third stall from the door," LiQui said. "Some sort of homicide happened in there and it smells like eighty sweaty jock pits."

"At least it's not eighty-one," I said as I undertook the walk of shame to the bathroom/SnackBox area. The bathrooms were backed into the farthest corner of the school, and there was only a good four feet in between the bathroom wall and the SPA fence. There was a big streetlight right above the structure, but it was still laid out in a way that, if you wanted to make out, it was only a matter of sliding between the bathroom and the fence. Everyone knew this, which was why no one looked in that space when they went to the bathroom.

I had the same intentions. There was nothing different about this bathroom trip—at least, that was what I believed until I saw a backpack with a white cover sticking out of it sitting by the fence gap. Confused, curious, and a little frustrated at the recklessness, I wanted to know what patron of mine was being so willy-nilly with my books after I'd said to be as careful as possible. Beyond all sense, I stepped off the designated make-out-free path and peeked around the forbidden corner.

Jack Lodenhauer was there, one hand pulling a PBR out of a twelve-pack sitting on the ground. I didn't know it was him at first—it was dark—but he was one of the shortest guys at LA, and his pointy hair was a silhouette that stuck into the darkness the same way it stuck into the light.

I stared at him for way too long, and before I had the sense to pull my head back around the corner, he turned.

Our eyes met and I jerked back, rushing into the women's bathroom, praying to God that Jack Lodey hadn't seen me and wondering why on earth he had one of my white covers, when I'd never checked one out to him. Probably Ashton. Or maybe Resi. Was Jack reading *Speak*?

I normally wasn't a germophobe, but the field bathrooms made me one. They were LA's weakness. No matter how hard the Maintenance and Operations department tried, they always looked like someone had intentionally peed on everything. Every surface had some sort of dampness on it, and the third stall was, as prophesied, home to some sort of unspeakable evil, so I walked all the way to the last stall. Then I made a toilet-seat cover out of toilet paper and did my best not to let anything but the soles of my shoes touch the floor.

After washing my hands, I stuck my head out the bathroom door, listening for any sign of Jack Lodey, and when I decided that the only thing I heard was the wind whipping through the fence, I speed-walked out of there.

I turned the corner and ran straight into Ashton. With the same backpack I'd seen by the bathrooms, the white cover now gone. Maybe it had been Ashton's all along.

"Sorry! Oh man, I'm—" He turned and saw it was me. When he did, his face soured and he looked irritated instead of apologetic.

"Am I a lemon?" I asked, the question flying out of my mouth before I could stop it. Did I not have a filter? What on earth?

"What? No. Sorry." His face softened as if the comment shamed him into being polite, which he didn't need to be after our last conversation. He looked back toward the bathrooms.

"I'm sorry," I said. "About this morning. I didn't mean . . . I didn't mean to pigeonhole you like that."

He shrugged. "I'm used to it. Actually . . . okay, I have a question for you."

I cocked my head.

He waited for a long few seconds, then waved me off with a "Never mind. It's stupid."

"What? No. You've got me curious now. You have to ask."

He frowned, but not in a mean way. It was a frown that said, *I wish I didn't have to ask this question at all.*

"Not to be creepy," he said, "but would you mind . . . pulling back a bit? Like, so we can talk without hungry ears around?"

We walked behind the bleachers, not completely out of eyesight, but enough that if anyone were to see us, we'd be suspicious. Lava lamps in a fancy furniture store. It stood out to me that I'd somehow wound up in both universally agreed "no-no" areas of LA football games in one night. I hadn't thought that starting a banned-book library was the type of thing that would bring me to such dark alleys and dangerous places.

"What's up?" I asked. "To what do I owe the pleasure of Ashton Bricks pulling me behind the bleachers?"

"Ha. Extra, extra! So," he started. "Uh, I've got this friend who's like . . . I don't know. Who's like . . . absolutely miserable with his life for completely valid reasons, but because of it, he's slowly destroying his life? And I don't really know what to do. But he's . . . they've started reading books to cope, I think. Do you have any book recs or something that could help? Me or him?"

Oh, Jack Lodenhauer. So not all was money, King Ranch trucks, and fancy shirts in Lodey land.

My thoughts must have shown on my face, because he shrugged and then laughed at my silence. "Why did I think this was a good idea? I knew where you stood this morning. We're not supposed to have problems. We're the rich kids. We've got it all. I don't want to miss the game. I'll see you later, Clara. Thanks."

He said it like a joke, but it wasn't. It was sharp as a knife edge and as gritty as sandpaper, stuffed with a heaviness, maybe from dealing with a lost friend, maybe from yet another disappointment that a person he'd thought would listen had written him off . . . again.

Maybe, just like the rest of the world.

I was the world.

And as soon as he walked away, it didn't feel great.


I couldn't watch dudes running around and grunting. I couldn't sit still. I kept thinking about Ashton. LiQui was super into the game, as was always the case, so I got up and decided to find Ashton and apologize. I wandered along the bleachers, looking for where the star-stars sat. I saw Resi and the rest of the crew, but not Jack and Ashton.

I'd decided to brave the bathroom area again when I saw Jack standing in the food line of the SnackBox. In that moment, the most unexpected thought came over me:

I needed to talk to Jack Lodenhauer.

I needed to apologize to him for being a jerk at Queso.

I didn't know why, all of a sudden, I felt the need to apologize to a star-star. Maybe it was because I felt like I owed Ashton? Maybe it was because my interactions with Ashton had made me realize that I wasn't as empathetic as I thought I was. Maybe it was because I realized that yelling someone out of Queso wasn't a thing that the book gods would ever stand for. Whatever the reason, I had to do it. It was as if the moment I had the thought, it imprinted itself into my DNA.

I took a deep breath, thinking of Levi and Joss and their grand kindness, and walked up to him.

"Jack?" I asked.

He ignored me.

"Jack?" I asked again, standing right in front of him. He looked at me, but said nothing.

"Look, I wanted to apologize for bitching you out of Queso. I just . . . yeah . . . I'm sorry. Please come back if you want."

He nodded.

"Oh, and, um, I'll hook you up with some books? I know some good ones that'll make you feel like you aren't alone. That you belong."

He looked up at me. "Why would you say that?"

Finally getting a response shocked me and I scrambled to recover. "I mean, not that you do feel like you're alone. I just . . . like, I don't feel like I belong half the time, and it's sort of a common feeling, so I thought maybe it'd be a good descriptive sentence to explain what sort of books they were? It wasn't a direct sentence or anything. Unless you don't feel like you belong, but I wouldn't know. So if you do or don't, I don't know. Just wanted to be clear on that. I don't—" I stopped myself, took a breath. "I think I can find a book you like. And I'd love to hear your thoughts on whatever book it is. You probably have a unique perspective."

Jack looked at me like I was an idiot. A pure-blood all-American idiot. I sighed.

"Well, sorry. I'll see you later."

I walked away. Feeling like the stupidest person on the face of the planet. The very feeling that I'd always felt around the star-stars, and I couldn't tell if it made me mad or made me feel like I actually was an all-American idiot.

Maybe both.

## ALL THE WRONG FIRES

The weekend passed, made up of, mostly, homework and Netflix with my dad. It was Monday and I shut the locker on three white-covered new copies of *Don't Tread on Me* I'd picked up at Bookies using my LitHouse bank account (it was a business expense!) and then walked toward Honors Lit. I turned down the hall, past the library, and, as if fate wanted me to feel my shortcomings, Ashton Bricks came toward me. He looked, for lack of a better description, not good. Rushed, his right shoe untied, his hair a flighty mess, but it was more that the air around him looked . . . burned. Like on a really really hot day, when you can see the heat waves rippling off tarmac.

I watched him, wondering if he was going to look up. I didn't know what I'd say if he did, but I didn't have to figure it out. He simply walked past me without a glance. I thought, then, how I might've broken him with the book I'd given him, *Speak*.

I was doing this thing with the Unlib where the point was to prove the books weren't garbage. Ashton, initially, had thought it was cool. A magical bridge of unpredictable awe and belief connected us. Maybe that was why he'd asked me about Jack? He'd thought I was a safe place, a harbor where he could winter for a minute, but then I wasn't. Did it matter that I'd given him *Speak*? How much did the giver represent the thing given? Especially since I'd stereotyped him twice, once after apologizing. How could I sell these books in my locker as life-changing if I was acting like every other Tom, Dick, and Harry? If I wasn't even taking into account the things the very "life-changing" book I was giving him had taught me?

Finally, thirty seconds after Ashton had passed me, I knew what I could've said.

I could've said, *Sorry*.

I turned to look for him, but he was gone. Probably on his way to Honors Lit. I slammed my locker shut, but before I could turn to leave, the Mav appeared in front of me. Blocking what seemed like the entire hall with his Mav mass. He held a white cover in his hand, presumably *Eleanor and Park*.

"Hey," he said.

"Hey, Mav," I said, not having the strength to deal with our past—well, more so his past with LiQui and what I felt about it. It didn't seem to matter as much when I was mad at myself for being a jerk.

He handed the white cover back to me. Had he really read it in five days?

"What did you think of it?" I asked.

"Of what?"

"The Louisiana Purchase, obviously."

"Oh, is that that new heist movie?"

"Cool. Want to check out another one?"

"Another book?"

"No. Another heist movie. This one's called *The Alaskan Purchase*."

"Dang. You have movies, too?"

"How did you talk LiQui into dating you?"

The Mav pulled up his shirt and showed me a six-pack of abs.

I sighed. "Yeah, that makes sense. Do. You. Want. To. Check. Out. Another. Book."

"Oh, yeah, for sure. I loved this one. It was a heartfelt exploration of the difficulties of coming into a relationship with very complex situational and socioeconomic contexts. Heartbreaking."

"I'm sorry, what?"

He pointed at the book in my hands. I looked at the book in shock, because on the front cover, he'd written something in red pen. I held it closer to my eyes.

*"He made her feel like more than the sum of her parts," and so did this book. Made me not think love was just the pits again.*

An "aw" started creeping up my throat, but then I realized he was talking about his breakup with LiQui. That one fire-truck-red line of ink, written on blizzard white, told me he hadn't left LiQui because "why not," but that he'd had some reason that neither LiQui nor I understood. Not only that, but he still hurt. There stood the Mav, who'd been for three years, in my mind at least, a six-pack with fancy hair, but then these newly conjured images of him danced in my head. Him and his grandma stalking

Instagram pictures of Jeff Goldblum, and another where he pulled his car over on some back country road because a snapping turtle was crossing ahead. Him reading *Eleanor and Park* and turning the pages like they mattered.

What was the Mav? What was Ashton?

I'd thought I knew, for so long. I'd thought I knew who the Mav was, but at that moment I didn't. Same with Ashton.

"So, what do you have?" the Mav asked.

"Well, what do you want?"

He smiled. "Everything."

So I gave him a brand-new copy of *Don't Tread on Me*, and then grabbed another copy, knowing that as soon as LiQui heard Mav was reading *DTOM*, she'd want to read it, too. I also grabbed copies of my fantastic four (*Speak, Catcher in the Rye, Perks of Being a Wallflower*, and *Don't Tread on Me*) to give to Jack at Honors Lit. I knew he wouldn't ask me for books—I'd probably already burned that bridge, if there'd ever been one—but Ashton was obviously worried about him and was asking for books *for* him, so I thought maybe it'd be a good gesture to give him all my favorites to start.

The prospect of having so many copies of *Don't Tread on Me* out in the world felt strange. I think because it was a weird thing to realize, you know? The communal aspect of books. They became so close to you, so ingrained in your blood, that it was like they became unpublished. The bar code, along with the memory of buying it along with five other duplicate copies, disappeared. And somewhere between the covers you'd start to think you were the only one who'd ever set eyes on the words, that there couldn't possibly have been another person that book spoke to as much as you.

As it had since it started, the banning showed up in my brain with its hulking frame and condescending wagging finger. Acting as a period to any happy thoughts I'd ever had about books. I sighed. Then I walked into Honors Lit, where Ms. Croft stood at the front writing *Todd v. Rochester Community Schools* on the blackboard.

I sat down next to Ashton and was pulling out all my stuff when I realized the room sounded like one big whisper. As if everyone had collectively decided that Honors Lit was the trading post of secrets. Everyone had decided it was okay to talk in class. I grabbed the white covers I'd picked for Jack, and I turned toward Ashton so I could have him pass them over when I saw that Jack was gone.

"Where is he? Is he okay?" I whispered.

Ashton shrugged, not giving me an answer.

"I was going to give him these," I said. "I checked them out to him and everything."

Ashton took them and quickly shoved them into his backpack, then said, "I'll get them to him."

I opened my mouth to apologize, this time I didn't even know what for, but before I could say anything, Ms. Croft started talking about the new court case she'd written on the board. This one involved a man who took a public school to court because *Slaughterhouse-Five* contained and referenced religious matters.

Suddenly I felt even more like circus trash. A half-eaten funnel cake. Soggy cotton candy. I felt very not like Joss and Levi, and that made me wonder. If I was over here hating people, being angry at ridiculous grown men pretending to have noble principles, did that matter for the Unlib? Did my dirt taint the Unlib in some way? I mean, *was* the Unlib just a power trip like Scott had said in the cafeteria on Friday? Was I power-tripping—like Mr.

Walsh but in the opposite direction? Did it matter if I was? On that thought, did it matter that I was telling people what to read? That I was handing books to Jack that I thought were beneficial? It felt like it did, even if I couldn't see how. But, the thing was, no one else was going to push Mr. Walsh, push Lupton, like this. And someone needed to be pushing. But the pushing wasn't why I felt bad; it was Ashton. Right?

I nodded. But, for some reason, I still felt like I was lying to myself.

## LONELY NOODLES

Second star to the right, straight on till morning, and there was the StuCab and me. Circus trash extraordinaire. I poked at the mac and cheese. Shoving one noodle from one place to another as everyone talked about Jack Lodey's drunken Friday night. Apparently, before he left the school parking lot, he ran his car over a lamppost and straight through the SPA fence. Then, somehow, his car still worked *and* he got it out and got an underage DUI on his way home. I didn't know if the latter was true. I'd only heard that some students had seen him pulled over. The rumor about the SPA fence and lamppost being totaled was definitely true. I saw the destruction when I was parking that morning.

I couldn't stop thinking that I'd seen it happen and done nothing. Seen the drinking. Seen the damage of it in Ashton's eyes, which was why the whispers bothered me, and, surely, they bothered the star-stars.

I looked over my shoulder at the star-star table. Of course Jack wasn't there. Ashton looked about the same as I did, hunched over his food, ignoring the banter of the rest of his friends. Watching Ashton feeling the same feelings I felt really made it hard not to stand up in the middle of the cafeteria, walk over to him, and say sorry right on the spot, but that wasn't how it worked at LA. Tables were realms, separated by moats filled with stares and castle walls built of insecurity. To walk up to one that wasn't yours, unless you were a preapproved social butterfly, would be as attention-getting as using an open-mic night at a bar to confess murder. It was so *panem et circenses.*

But . . . then I saw him push a noodle across his plate.

I looked down at the lone noodle on the side of my own plate, far, far away from its cheesy brothers and sisters. It was almost symbolic. There were two isolated noodles in this very cafeteria, and somehow, knowing that made my

noodle feel less isolated. Like, sure, the noodle was separated from the collective mac and cheese, but it wasn't
unique in its separation. It wasn't special. I wasn't special.
Having hurt feelings didn't make me an ogre living in iso-
lation; if anything, it connected me to Ashton. Two objects
not alike in form but alarmingly the same in essence.

What was the most un–*panem et circenses*, circus-trash
thing to do?

I grabbed my fork, stabbed my isolated noodle, stood
up, and set my course toward the star-star table.

## NON-LONELY NOODLES

*Until that moment, she had never thought she could do it. Never thought*
*she would be brave enough, or scared enough, or desperate enough to dare.*

—Neil Gaiman, *Neverwhere*

I ignored the eyes.

I ignored the whispers.

I ignored the circus.

All so I could put a noodle on some kid's plate.

I walked up to Ashton, fork with noodle. Ashton looked
up at me, more confused than mad. I felt some heat from
the other star-stars, their diamond-drill-bit eyes running
all over me. Wondering why such a plebeian would dare
to make contact with the celestial shores. But then, I

wondered if it even was that dramatic. Maybe they were looking at me the same way the rest of the school was.

"I'm sorry," I said. "Really. I'm sorry."

He sat up a little straighter, gave me a quick smile, and then said, "What's with the noodle?"

I popped it off the tines, placed it on his plate next to his, then sat awkwardly by him. "There's no time in this life for lonely noodles."

Resi turned to me, putting her back to the other star-stars. "Hey, Clara, I have your book. I can give it to you now?"

I shook my head. "No. Not in front of the paparazzi," I said, motioning vaguely behind me.

"Okay. I'll stop by your locker later," Resi said. "Before I go home. To drop it off."

I nodded. "I'll see you then."

"Thanks for making my noodle less lonely," Ashton said.

I laughed. "Don't say that to every girl you meet."

He cocked his head, confused, and stood up and walked away wondering how different the day would've been if we'd been served corn instead of mac and cheese.

Back at my table, I sat down and ate the mac and cheese in giant bites, shoving as many noodles as I could onto my fork tines. Cramming them on until they were popping off. I didn't want them to be alone.

"Uh," Scott said, "you're just going to eat your mac and cheese and not talk about the travesty you committed in the eyes of God and everyone else?"

I groaned. "Can you talk about Resi or something?"

"Can you talk about why you took a solitary noodle to Ashton Bricks?" LiQui asked.

"Does it matter? You would've done the same thing."

LiQui's *report* face appeared. "C, you know I wouldn't have. You also know that if you don't want to wake up with your hand in a cup of water every night for the next month, you need to spill."

So I spilled the basics.

Ashton was nice.

I was not.

The end.

# THE LIGHT SWITCH

Levi and I could hear the man's joints creak as he walked down the stairs, torch in hand. "These lights," he said, pointing toward the old can lights in the ceiling. "Haven't worked for at least thirty years. They used to flicker, you see. I meant to fix them. Never did. So I turned them off. A flickering light is worse than none at all. But then I left for the war. One thing after another, you know. When I came back, I didn't want to see this place. Took me fifteen years to even open the door. There is so much down here and most of it I can't even recall."

"How come you didn't fix them when you finally came around?" Levi asked.

"I couldn't remember where the switch was! Still can't. I've had this idea that, if I found the switch by pure happenstance, I'd fix them and do this place justice. Let fate decide if I should throw myself back into the war. Over this way, I think."

*"Well, if you ever do find the switch,"* Levi said, *"we'd love to include any books you have in our library."*

*"Hundreds, at least," the old man said wearily. "Maybe more."*

*We followed the man into a damp basement. Dark as soot. Full to the brim with dusty boxes and nondescript objects. If it weren't for the old man's torch, we'd be blind.*

*"I found this one in a foxhole after the Battle of Tulsa. Grabbed it and shoved it into my rucksack. There's a few bloodstains, but they make it more poetic."*

*He handed us a black book, its covers worn, bending, creased. All the signs of love. I reached out to take it; the old man pulled back. "You swear to me that this will be cared for?"*

*I nodded. "Yes."*

*He extended his hand again, shaking. It took just as much bravery for him to give us this book as it did for us to carry it home. My fingers wrapped around its spine.*

*"Thank you," I said. "Thank you."*

*"Ah, I see this was meant to be."*

*I frowned, and, beating Levi to the question, I asked, "How so?"*

*He smiled, toothy, wiry. "I believe I just found the light switch."*

—Lukas Gebhardt, *Don't Tread on Me*

\* \* \*

"Make him start on *Catcher*? Well . . . no, maybe *Perks* if he wants to be ready for Queso," I said to Ashton. He'd come with Resi to drop off her copy of *Speak*. "It's a How to Survive Humanity book, which sounds sort of like what he needs? Well, I guess both of those books are How to Survive Humanity books. I don't know—I just hope they help."

"Me too. I tell you what—I won't make him start on *Speak*," Ashton said. "That one's a slayer."

Resi held out her copy of *Speak*. On the cover was a quote written in a pretty ink scrawl. *I found bravery here.*

I read it once. Twice. Then looked at her. "That's beautiful."

Sure.

Maybe I needed a better reason for the Unlib, but, really, was it wrong to want to prove to Mr. Walsh that books mattered? That quote was the best I'd gotten thus far. How could you not be moved by that?

"It was a great book," she said.

"Want something else?"

She considered for a moment, then shook her head. "No, I think I'm all right for now."

With such a profound quote on the cover, the fact that she didn't want to read anything else was almost devastating, but, being the nonconfrontational Clara I was, I nodded and closed the locker.

## MORE ATTEMPTS TO FIGURE OUT
## WHAT TO SPEAK ABOUT AT
## THE FOUNDERS SCHOLARSHIP DINNER

- From Old and Busted to New Hotness: How to Update a Library (HINT: PLANTS)
- Tiny Little Libraries and How to Feed Them
- Building Bridges with Books (NICE! Bridges)
- Bringing Books to Everyone
- How to Stab Your School Librarian in the Back
- Gathering Lonely Noodles
- Why Is Everything So Complicated?
- Maybe People Are More Complex Than You Think
- You Know What? Give the Scholarship to Someone Who Can Come Up With Something Worthwhile to Talk About

## RUNNING ON BANANA-MUFFIN FUMES

The week blurred by in a hubbub filled with homework and fielding texts for the Unlib what seemed like every hour. I guessed that between the Mav, Ashton, Resi, LiQui, the StuCab, and Mr. Caywell there was a lot of word of mouth going around. A lot more than I'd thought would ever happen. There was so much Unlib to do that as I drove to school that Tuesday, thinking about how puffy and crammed the day would be with Unlib hustle, I wondered how I was going to get everything done.

Also, another problem with that morning: right before I left for school, my period hit me with its full rage, and it was hard to not want everything to die.

As usual, I got to school early and went straight to the

library. I'd promised Mr. Caywell I'd finally start organizing the processing room. It was the last thing I wanted to
do, but Mr. Caywell wasn't a person I could bail on. Why?
Because I was actively stabbing him in the neck with my
banned book–shaped knife of betrayal, and because he'd
done so much for me over the last three years, including
letting me borrow his car for a day when mine died, that I
couldn't say no. Ever.

As I was working out a labeling system for the shelves,
he popped open the door.

"I stopped by your TLL by the Riverwalk the other day.
I didn't see a single one of our books in there. They must
be moving quick."

I whirled around to see if he was being snarky or not.
When I saw sincerity, a pure excitement that the books
had found good homes, I decided to shove my betrayal
knife all the way down to his toenails because I was a
horrible person.

"Uh, yeah! I put like five in there."

"Wow," he said. Nodding. Then, turning to sit in his
chair to go through emails: "That's incredible. Hey, speaking of banned things, there are a couple of donated copies

of *The Chocolate War* right there that you need to put in your libraries."

"Oh, okay. Yeah, I'll do that. For sure. I mean, not right now—I have to do some work—but I'll do it, no problem. Maybe I'll put them in the TLL near the Riverwalk! Full circle, right?"

"Why are you panic talking?" Mr. Caywell asked, not even turning around to ask.

"What? I'm not panic talking! I mean, I'm talking. But not panicking. So I can't be panic talking."

"You're most certainly panic talking."

"Maybe you make me nervous with all your standing and hovering."

He turned in his chair. "What?"

"What?"

"No. What is going on?"

I sighed and attempted to think of an excuse. "Fine! I just . . . I don't like *The Chocolate War*. I think it's overstated."

I couldn't remember the last time I'd read *The Chocolate War*—years ago. I didn't remember much of it outside of the quote "Do I dare disturb the universe?" and that I'd added the name Leon to my Names of Boys to Never Trust Until Proven Wrong list. But, if you needed a critique in a pinch, *overstated* and *understated* were adjectives that worked perfectly and sounded intelligent enough to make it seem like you'd thought about it.

"'Overstated'?" he said, then shrugged. "It's been years since I read that book, so I have no feet to stand on in this argument. You're a librarian. It doesn't matter if you like it. Add it anyway."

I saluted. "Yes, sir!"

Doing my best to forget the fact that I was becoming a worse person literally every second, I took a breath, stared at the overwhelming number of old boxes filled with dona- tions, and got to work, ignoring my screaming uterus to the best of my ability. I labeled three sets of black metal shelves and had gotten into a good and easy groove of going through box after box, putting things in piles to sort, throwing out anything that wasn't a book, when the bell rang. I cursed, grabbed my bag and the copies of *The Choc- olate War* on top of it, and bolted out of the processing room.

"You're late!" Mr. Caywell said.

"You're really helpful, you know that?" I yelled, running

out of the library. I turned the corner; the halls were empty. And there I was again, running from the library to Honors Lit.

"Ms. Evans," I heard from behind me, "I must ask, why are you yelling?"

I turned, but didn't stop walking backward. "Sorry, Mr. Walsh; I was talking to Mr. Caywell."

"You realize you're late for class, yes?"

*No, Mr. Walsh, I was running off the banana muffin I had for breakfast.*

"Yes," I said, looking down at my shoes, trying to hide my frustration, only to see that I had two banned books clutched in my hands, exposed for the world and its mother to see. I spun back around, almost tripping over my feet. "Gotta get to class, Principal Walsh, sorry!"

"Tut-tut-tut," he said. "Stop, please."

I did, but I didn't turn around. I just looked over my shoulder. My heartbeat thrummed in the silence. "Yes, Principal Walsh?"

"Please come to my office for a moment, Ms. Evans."

## LOOP-DE-LOOPHOLES

Principal Walsh sat on a fancy ergonomic mesh office chair behind his desk like it was a throne. It wasn't even that nice a chair. As far from a throne as a toothbrush was from a car. He wasn't even that nice a person. He sucked and his desk chair sucked.

*"The Chocolate War,"* he said, flipping the book over. Scanning it. No. Not scanning it—remembering it. Reliving it. His eyes stayed fixed on the cover for longer than a simple scan. Most people wouldn't know the difference, but I knew. I saw it all the time in the library.

Whatever remembrance he'd had, it left as he tossed the book onto his desk. "Can you tell me why you're carrying prohibited media around campus? You do realize that having this media is against school policy."

At first, I thought the best thing I could say was also the truest thing—*I was getting rid of them for Mr. Caywell*—but I wondered if that would get him in trouble. Surely a staff member giving a student banned books, regardless of the circumstances, wasn't kosher. Even though Mr. Caywell probably would've wanted me to tell the truth, I couldn't throw him under the bus. It'd give me circus-trash points I didn't need. But if I couldn't tell the truth, what should I say?

The conversation LiQui and I had had in the library popped into my head. The one in which she'd told me exactly how a meeting like this would go. Suddenly, what had been a very inconvenient situation a few seconds prior turned into an experimental gift.

"So these books are banned?" I asked.

He went stiff. As if he didn't want a stray head nod to betray some sort of vague political boundary he'd memorized.

"There is a list of prohibited media in the student handbook, and, of course, having prohibited media is against school policy."

"Okay," I said, because I was A-game Clara, "but do you mind if I ask why?"

His eyebrows, with that one eyebrow hair that was freakishly long, fell flat. His nostrils elongated into ovals. Everything about him lengthened in bother. "Because it's not currently conducive to your learning conditions."

"Oh," I said, feigning understanding. "Okay, well, I guess I'll go read the handbook, then, just so I know what books are banned."

"Yes! Which media is prohibited is something all students should know. In fact, the student handbook should be read frequently, with conviction. Considering your apologetic state, I'll let you off with a warning for now, Ms. Evans, but if I catch you again, I'll unfortunately have to give you a strike."

I forced a smile. "Right. I'll . . . check out the handbook to see what books are banned."

"All good student citizens should be aware of what media is prohibited! Ciao, Clara Evans."

He walked out from behind his desk, grabbed the two copies of *The Chocolate War*, and walked out of his office, leaving me there. Alone. Without a late slip.

I stood and glared at the desk. "You're literally the worst desk I've ever seen."

And with that, I left, wondering what I'd say to Ms. Croft for being late. Again. Probably the truth. Maybe if I told her the truth she'd get mad and inspirational again, and I could draw some strength from her.

I walked to Honors Lit. There were two noticeable differences in the classroom. The first was that Jack Lodenhauer was still not in his chair. The second was that Ms. Croft was not standing at the front of the classroom; in fact, she wasn't standing anywhere. Instead there was a woman with short gray hair and a pencil skirt. She certainly didn't have magnolia-flower tattoos, and it was highly plausible she'd borrowed her hair from a seventies workout video.

I took a step back and checked the room number. The room was right. I looked for Ashton. Sure enough, he was sitting in his normal spot.

"I'm sorry, can I help you?" The teacher paused.

I looked at everyone for some sort of explanation, but none came.

"Uh, is this Honors Lit?"

"Yes, and you would've known that if you were here on time."

"Right," I said, sliding into my chair. "I got caught up with a project for the library."

"Tardiness is tardiness," she said simply, and then got back to her blackboard, which had a dusty scrawl about the benefits of reading *Alice in Wonderland* in Latin.

"What circus trash is this?" I whispered to Ashton while Ms. PencilySkirtSkirt was writing a novel on the blackboard. I reached into my backpack to grab my binder and found a white cover that I was pretty sure I'd checked out to Hanna Chen a while back. I couldn't even remember her giving it back to me. That's how crazy it was. I was literally forgetting parts of my day.

"I don't know," he said. "But I guess she's our circus trash for the rest of the semester. She's claiming she's our new teacher."

"Uhhh . . . where's Ms. Croft?"

## MCSKIRTYLACKOFJOY AND
## ALL THE OTHER STUFF

*In the swaying ether of the goldenrod, night had no space to settle within the yellow fractals. Desiring the same effect, in her never-ending search for simplicity, Lila considered this for days when the simplest thing to have done would have been to not consider it at all.*

—Lukas Gebhardt, *A House of Wooden Windows*

"What is happening?" I asked the StuCab. "This school is falling apart, and it's *not* because of the beef."

"You talking about the teacher they let go?" LiQui asked.

I nearly jumped off my seat. "They let Ms. Croft go? It wasn't like a 'take a break, go away for the summer, go upstate' sort of thing?"

"Gone," LiQui said. "Official announcement to staff was something about 'differences in policy opinion.'"

"She was my Honors Lit teacher!" I sat back down and buried my head in my hands. "Why does senior year suck so bad?"

"I had Ms. Croft for English Comp when I was the freshest man; she was great. A little scary, but great," Scott said. "Also, Clara, that *Perks* book is amazing."

I rubbed my eyes. "LiQui, did you give *Perks* to Scott instead of reading it yourself?"

LiQui grimaced. "Scott, you're killing me. I told you you could read it as long as you didn't tell Clara."

"Ugh, you're such a book jerk, LiQui. Sorry, Scott, no offense, I really am glad you like it. But LiQui should be the one reading it."

I looked at the star-star table, still devoid of Jack Lodenhauer, though I knew that if I listened to the conversations around me, he'd be everywhere. We were all circus trash, I guessed. We all pretended we were above a good train wreck, but most of us would derail a train with our own hands if it'd help us forget, even for a minute, that we were still sore from walking away from our own wreckage.

I vowed then that I wouldn't utter another bad vowel or consonant about Jack Lodenhauer.

"Who's teaching Honors Lit now?" LiQui asked.

"Ms. Pencily McSkirtyLackofJoy, but that's not important," I said, remembering my visit to Mr. Walsh's office. "LiQui, you need to show me the banned-book list."

She frowned. "Did we not have that discussion already?"

"Oh, imagine that. I guess I'll have to go back and talk to Mr. Walsh about the fact that I still haven't seen the list of 'prohibited media.'"

"Did you get caught with a white cover?"

"No. I got caught with banned donations that Mr. Caywell was giving me for the TLLs."

LiQui shook her head. "Dude pulled you in for donations?"

"Yeah, I was in his office for a chunk of Honors Lit this morning, so you can imagine my surprise, my shock, when McSkirty was in class instead of Ms. Croft."

"Have you heard anything else about Ms. Croft?" Scott asked.

LiQui shook her head. "Nothing outside of the fact that there were 'differences in policy.'"

"Dang, this school is getting turbulent," I said. "I didn't realize it was so political around here." I shoved the last bit of food in my mouth, stood up, and started collecting my stuff. "I've got some books to hustle. I'll see everyone later."

"Let me know what happens with Prince Walsh," LiQui said. "Let me know if you need backup."

"I will—I'm about to go see him again."

"You'll be great. You're the female warrior, more badass version of Levi and Joss."

"I wish," I said. "I'm not Levi and Joss. I'm just Clara."

LiQui scoffed. "Levi and Joss were only Levi and Joss until they were Levi and Joss."

I pointed to her. "You're reading *DTOM*?"

She nodded. "Keeping up with the Mav's reading list, or, really, Jeff Goldblum's book club."

## FIT IN LITTLE, BELONG MUCH

It was happening. I was getting quotes. A lot of them.

*Beautiful. I needed beautiful.*

*Jack L is Hott.*

*Fit in little. Belong much.*

*So far, my years have only ever asked questions.*

Despite the second quote, people writing things on the white covers was downright moving in ways I hadn't thought it'd be. Maybe simply getting people to write their love of a book down was worth more than having proof. Maybe it was a movement. Maybe it meant something different, and I just didn't know what that was yet. I kept rereading the quotes. Over and over. They made checking a book out exciting because I was excited to remember them.

What a way to live, being excited to remember.

## NOT A WALSH TO BE FOUND

*It's like the smarter you are, the more things can scare you.*

—Katherine Paterson, *Bridge to Terabithia*

I stood in Mr. Walsh's office, but there wasn't a single Mr. Walsh to be found. The school was fresh out. I hung there for a few minutes, thinking maybe the prodigal principal would return, but seconds flew by and I was running out of time before my next class. I'd already been late to one that day, and I didn't feel like being surprised by another pencil-skirted Komodo dragon. If any of my other classes had changes in teachers, I wanted to find out without being ridiculed in front of the whole class.

A little defeated, I walked out of his office.

I couldn't help but wonder if I was witnessing his trick.

It was common knowledge he walked the halls a lot, but maybe it wasn't because he wanted to keep tabs on the students. Maybe if he didn't sit in his office, he wouldn't have to deal with things like me. Maybe that was why LiQui had such an involved student-body position, why the StuCab existed at all. Maybe the entire system of LA had been set up to make it so complicated and confusing to get anywhere that we would all let things go when they came up.

Maybe that was why Mr. Caywell pushed back with the gusto of a sneeze. Maybe the people who pushed back, like Ms. Croft, ended up like Ms. Croft. Maybe LA's entire administration system was built around "students don't care enough to fight this." So they found the ones who would care—LiQui—and they put them in positions they could control. A process of eliminating the dissent. Not that LiQui didn't rock at being StuPres or that she didn't do awesome things. She did and she was way too good for LA. But maybe StuCab was a way to give the student body a placebo feeling of control. A way for the administration to run a school to ensure they get their hard tuition cash and then herd us through our four years without incident. *Panem et circenses*. Money to buy the bread. Just enough we-care-about-what-you-thinks to make students feel entertained. It was hard to not see the emptiness of everything once you read *DTOM*. To be honest, some days having read *DTOM* felt less enlightening and more demoralizing.

Focus. Knowledge. Impact. What if those principles were second to Contain, Control, and some third word that served equally as an antithesis? And maybe also started with *C*?

These thoughts were so stunning, so conspiratorial, I stopped in the middle of the hall.

Maybe Mr. Walsh just . . . couldn't sit still. Maybe I was seeing politics where politics didn't exist. Maybe Mr. Walsh wanted to reach ten thousand steps on his Fitbit. I was taking the leadership in all the dystopian novels, including *Don't Tread on Me*, and injecting it unfairly into LA.

Right?

## QUESTIONS FROM STRANGERS ABOUT STRANGERS

That night, there was a wall of texts asking me for books.

This time from people I knew of but had never interacted with. A.k.a. Mr. Caywell/StuCab referrals. But there was one text that had to do with books from someone I did know. And that was the most mind-consuming of them all. A conversation that, going into the new week, I couldn't shake.

**Ashton** [6:56 PM] So, I gave Jack those books. I told him they were from you. How do they fit into all this? Why did you choose them?

**Me** [6:56 PM] Outside of just that they are my favs?

Well, Holden and Charlie deal with a lot of things.

I thought they'd be helpful in that regard. Like, this line from Catcher:

"'Did you ever get fed up?' I said. 'I mean did you ever

get scared that everything was going to go lousy unless

you did something?'"

**Ashton** [7:01 PM] Yeah.

Also, is Queso Book Club tomorrow?

**Me** [7:01 PM] Queso too long for you?

Yeah. We shoot for every other week. You going to come?

**Ashton** [7:01 PM] Yeah. Jack, too.

**Me** [7:02 PM] This might be a weird question.

Because we don't really know each other.

Are you okay?

Is Jack okay?

**Me** [7:10 PM] Ashton?

# A CELEBRATORY ANNOUNCEMENT

To: All Students, All Faculty, All Parents

From: m.walsh@luptonacademy.edu

Subject: A Celebratory Announcement


Dear Lupton Family,

It is my pleasure to write to you today and tell you that after many years of negotiations, the Lupton Academy board has reached an agreement to purchase the Stringer and Peerless Alliance area behind Lupton Academy. The purchase was made possible, in part, by a generous donation from an anonymous donor.


Though, at this time, the sale of the SPA land will make a much-needed expansion of LA possible, there is still much to do. Contracts to be signed. Permits and planning. A fund-raising campaign. Our community will have the opportunity to play a big part in the future, both physical and directional, of Lupton Academy.

Sincerely,

Principal Milton Walsh

## TOMAYTO, TOMAHTO, PROHIBITED, BANNED

*Graphite scratched on paper. The old world strained to hear; the new world simply moved closer.*

—Lukas Gebhardt, *Don't Tread on Me*

I showed up early Wednesday morning, battling mist, fog, and spilled coffee on my pants, to track down Mr. Walsh before he started his daily dodging act. I walked by the SPA fence, it and the lamppost still busted and bent, the tap dance of rain on my jacket increasing in speed and sound. There was so much fog that I couldn't see the rickety SPA houses I'd spent years looking at and hearing about. And, of course, I couldn't help thinking about the amount of money the anonymous donor had dropped for them when all I wanted was for my car to stop making coughing noises when I turned it off. And maybe a pair of pants that didn't have an Antarctica-shaped coffee stain near my crotch.

After a fuss so ritualistic and ancient, and downright historically embedded, the donation had been sudden. SPA and LA had been going back and forth for years, even before Principal Walsh had fluttered into the picture, and suddenly we had a donor swooping in from the ether with the millions needed to expand LA? I might have been barn-raised, but at least I hadn't been born yesterday. It didn't take much of a brain to figure out that some whispers, a compromise, and two hands shaking in a corner had gotten us here. A sixty-seven-and-a-half-million-dollar game of footsie under a table.

My only question was, *What did you sell, Mr. Walsh?*

God, it was sad. Questioning everything. All the time. It was exhausting tapping on everything thinking it was solid wood and learning it was veneer. I walked back toward campus, wishing I could cram all the fog in an old shopping bag and toss it in the trash. Fog days were the worst. It was like as soon as I swallowed a pinch of mist I became a broody lump despite any attempt at being anything but. On that misty paver path, even past the roundabout, there were no birds singing. The fresh smell of rain was drowned out by the massive globs of rainwater, which now hurled themselves straight at my face, forgoing my hood altogether.

I slogged through puddles and clumps of grass clippings that were wet-stuck to the pavers, hitting my rain boots on the doorframe before walking inside Lupton Hall. The only good news was that the coffee Crotcharctica was gone. Instead my pants looked like I'd pulled them out of a kiddie pool. Wet and splattered with grass.

Everything was quieter than normal, but mostly because the rain was louder than normal. How that worked, I didn't know, but it seemed symbolic of the day.

I practiced what I'd say. Saying it in my head over and over and over. Motor memory almost took me past his office, my feet marching on autopilot straight toward the library. I stopped, then took a few deep breaths, brushed the leftover grass off my pants, then went inside. His door was open, but only by the tiniest of slivers. He was inside— so was his ugly desk—so that was good. What was not good was that he was on the phone. And, for reasons we've already established, I listened in on the conversation.

"Yes. Yes, that sounds good. We'll see him soon. Glad we could work it out. Mm-hmm. Yes. Great. Thank you so much." He hung up the phone, and I waited a few seconds before knocking so it didn't seem like I'd been listening. A good command of sneaking is crucial to even the most innocent of plans.

"Who is it?"

"It's Clara Evans."

"Ah, Clara Evans." He opened the door wide, stuck his head out to see if his assistant was sitting at her desk, which she wasn't, and nodded toward the hall. "Let's talk in the hall, shall we?"

I nodded and we stepped outside.

"Mr. Walsh, I read the student handbook to see about the banned books?"

His eyes deepened, but his face remained static; his features, including that one freakishly long eyebrow hair, uncharacteristically still. "The prohibited media, yes."

I tossed up my hands in a show of exhaustion. Of pure confuddlement. "I looked everywhere, but there wasn't a list. There was a statement saying to check with your student-body president for a list, so I did, and she said she didn't have one, so I'm not really sure what to do?"

He shoved his hands in his pockets. "Ah, well, uh, only use the school library when on campus. If it's in the school library, then it's not banned. Prohibited, I mean. Very simple. Takes the guesswork out of it for you."

It was so obvious he'd never gotten to this point with a student that he was off his script. His predetermined buzzwords and cleverly crafted vagaries were empty.

"Okay, but that's still not helpful. If I don't know what's banned, I can end up with something on my record simply because I brought it on campus and didn't even know it was a problem. Can you post the list somewhere?"

"Oh, well. Well. Well, warnings are typically given to students if they bring anything prohibited on campus. It's not an immediate strike. You've even experienced this exact sort of situation. Nothing to worry about. Now, I must get back to work. I have a lot to work out with the SPA purchase. Exciting, isn't it?"

"Mr. Walsh, I don't think—"

"*Principal* Walsh. Ciao, Ms. Evans! Let me know if you have any more questions!"

"I do have—"

He walked back into his office and closed the door. I heard a telltale click. Locking me out.

I stood there for a few minutes. Just staring at the door. Eventually I took my broody-lump self to the library and did more work on the processing room. I set a timer on my phone to yell at me a full ten minutes before Honors Lit so I didn't get carried away.

## LEST YOU BE CIRCUS TRASH

*Destroying things is much easier than making them.*

—Suzanne Collins, *The Hunger Games*

I arrived to Honors Lit five minutes early to make up for the last disaster, but I wasn't the only one who'd come back from the edge of the world. I saw him as soon as I walked in, which was saying something, because there wasn't much that could compete with the bright, highlighter-orange pencil skirt (I had to give her this one tiny, tiny thing: at least she was repping orange highlighters) standing at the front of the classroom.

Jack Lodenhauer sat next to Ashton as if it was nothing but a Wednesday. Sitting. Just sitting. As if he hadn't gotten an underage DUI. Hadn't been suspended. Somehow, he was there. I got a warning for something I didn't even know about, but, in a week and a half, he came back from alcohol on campus, damaging school property *while* drunk, *and* getting an underage DUI. The last kid who got busted for drinking during a football game didn't come back for a month. LA has a war against student drinking almost as intense as the one against student reading.

I admit, I stood in the doorway longer than I should've, and I knew it, but I was attempting to convince myself of the vow I'd made.

*Not a word about Jack Lodey or his deeds, Clara Evans, lest you be circus trash.*

*Not a word.*

But in the same manner as she greeted me last time, Skirty SkirtSkirt made a very aggressive *come in and sit down* motion. The recipe—the gloom, me being a broody lump, the period, the confusion, the attempt at not being a jerk, the time limit the doorframe apparently had—all of it made her movements louder than the class-wide scolding she'd given me the first time, and words were coming out of my mouth before I could stop them.

"Who the hell are you even?" I asked. "Where's Ms. Croft?"

Yes.

I asked a teacher, without a single note of gentleness or respect in my voice, "Who the hell are you?"

In my defense, my pants were really, really, really cold from the air-conditioning, and that alone would make anyone snippy.

## ALL-AMERICAN IDIOT

I was back in Mr. Walsh's office. It was my new house. I'd been here so many times that I began to think maybe his desk wasn't as ugly as I'd initially thought. The place was one step up from my barn.

He stared at me, wordless and near blinkless; it all felt like a play. It was as if he put on the *I'm not angry, just disappointed* demeanor like he'd put on a coat. With enough sugar for me to assume that he wasn't actually disappointed. You typically didn't have to act like you were something unless you weren't that something in the first place.

"Third time I've seen you this week, Ms. Evans," he said. "You've never been an issue until this year—what's going on?"

I didn't know how to respond to that. I'd graduated from "contained brainwash-ee" to "issue" simply because I'd talked to him about a nonexistent policy he said was a policy. What a thrill.

He took my silence and paid me back with more "acting disappointed." "I'm going to give you a strike for this one. Swearing and yelling at a teacher."

"I didn't yell at her," I said. "I asked her who she was after she'd been unnecessarily mean to me for the second time. Who is she?" I asked. "She just showed up. Where did Ms. Croft go? Administration hasn't said a single thing about it."

"That's because what happens behind the scenes doesn't concern students. Your job is to learn. Our job is to administer. We trust you to do yours. You should trust us to do ours. Focus. Knowledge. Impac—"

"Yes, Mr. Walsh. I get it."

He shook his head, ruffled from being interrupted in his script.

"Would you like to tell your parents about this incident or do I have to call them?"

I thought it funny. My parents were going to get a

call from my principal, telling them that their daughter, whose biggest flub to date had been being late to a class because she'd poured chicken-noodle soup on a binder, had cussed out a teacher. It was an easier way for them to get an update about my life than any other option, I guessed. I hadn't been very open since school started. I'd had a continual lack of desire to tell them anything since I'd started the Unlib.

I laughed. "You know what? Can you call them?"

"I don't think this is funny, Ms. Evans. Why do you?"

Suddenly, an epiphany struck me.

That morning, when Mr. Walsh had been on the phone, he'd said, "We'll see him soon." And then, Jack Lodey.

Sitting in Honors Lit.

Very soon.

So that was it. The Lodenhauers had bought SPA for LA to get Jack back in school. Would there be anything on his record? Even if that wasn't the reason the Lodenhauers had bought SPA, I'm sure it was a side benefit. What did that mean? Did it matter? If Jack was living above the law, did that matter? Maybe? If that was really how this school played, we were all going day in and day out being duped into believing our voices mattered. And that our learning helped us craft how they mattered. And that we could change our surroundings. That we could have "impact." What do you do in a place where all the gears that make it work behind the scenes have rusted over? What do you do in a place that tells you over and over that you matter, but once you take a step into the open to try to matter, you're pushed back into your cage?

"Because this is weird. It's all weird," I said, and I wasn't sure if my answer was for him or for myself.

Mr. Walsh pursed his lips, then spent a good minute or so silently scribbling on a document that would go in my "file." I was a criminal now. Maybe it had all been a plan of my subconscious. Distract the principal by swearing at a teacher; then I'd be the girl who swore at teachers, not the girl who was running a black-market book op. Very rarely had those two problems been connected to each other in lab studies.

I sighed, listening to the scratch of writing. Wishing for the day to be over. Dreading leading Queso that night, as I hadn't even gotten around to rereading *Perks*. It was funny how little time you had to read when you were busy helping other people read.

Strangely, the part of the day I was least dreading? Going home to my parents.

What a plot twist.

## MOJOVATION

*And this you can know—fear the time when Manself will not suffer and die for a concept, for this one quality is the foundation of Manself, and this one quality is man, distinctive in the universe.*

—John Steinbeck, *The Grapes of Wrath*

I walked into Mojo and straight into a group of people all clustered in front of the door looking clueless and confused, blocking me from getting to the queso part of the book club. The people part I could take or leave. In my defense, the day had been fairly miserable, so I was holding on to any smaller beauty I could find. On that particular day, it was queso.

Standing among the confused, I realized that the

massive group of people were *my* people. The normal Que-soians, plus Ashton, Jack, StuCab, LiQui, and (surprise!) about half the kids from Honors Lit, and (double surprise!) Ms. Croft.

"Uhhh," I said. "Whoa?"

"Yeah," LiQui said. "You're welcome."

"For?"

She held out her arms. "I emailed Ms. Croft and asked her to show tonight. Also hit your class up. I'm not finding answers in contract-law research, so I figured, why not get the dirt from the lady who was fired?"

"Why didn't you tell me?" I said, groaning. "I'm not mentally prepared!"

"You were too busy swearing at teachers? You weren't even at lunch. What gives?"

"A. Fair. B. I had too many books to hustle. C. We can talk about that later. So, we have like fifteen people for tonight?"

"When I come, I bring mass. You're welcome."

"Okay, lay off, Maui." I sighed. "We need more space."

And we wouldn't find that at Mojo, so I guessed that meant moving away from queso.

No queso.

I was fresh out of smaller beauty.

"We've gotta go to Bookies," I said. "They have a big room in their basement. It's only ten minutes from here."

"I'll drive because we need to talk about you swearing at teachers," LiQui said.

I looked toward the door, knowing in my heart I had to leave quesoless, but trying to figure out if there was a way to beat the burrito line. Maybe all that was left was drastic action. Dive over the counter and stick my whole fist in the queso container and run out the door? What was the point of dignity if you didn't have queso? A fist covered in cheese was better than dignity by a long shot.

I cupped my hands around my mouth. "Okay, everyone. Uh, we're too big a group for here. Not, like, fat, but in collective size. Does that make sense? We need to migrate like birds. Let's make like the birds and head to Bookies. I mean, make like the birds and migrate. To the bookstore. To Bookies." I took a big breath as if I was in the middle of a workout. "Let's go to Bookies. Everyone know where that is? Yeah. It's on Main Street. Okay. Let's go."

"Clara," Ms. Croft said as I held the door open for all

the Quesoians. "I hope it was okay I came. You seem surprised."

I shrugged. "I'm not surprised I'm surprised."

Ms. Croft looked at me blankly.

"Sorry, it's been a long day. It's fine that you came. Seriously."

"Okay, thank you," she said, walking toward her car. "I'm excited to hear how things are going for you. I'll see you at Bookies."

Ashton held back from the crowd. Jack hung with him too. Then, when the last person was out of the door, Ashton leaned over and said, "Is this a drug front? Be honest."

"Who even knows anymore. I'll see y'all at Bookies."

I walked to LiQui's green Isuzu Rodeo, and, in order to get into the passenger seat, I had to go through the rear passenger door and then climb over the center console. I'd sat in the back before instead of putting in all the work to get to the front, and it always felt like an awkward mom/Uber situation. However, this time, as I crawled to the front, my foot slid off the console and wedged into the no-man's-land slice of space between it and the front seat.

My momentum carried me forward, and I fell headfirst into the cavity below the glove compartment, an arch of shame, foot in the seat, head on the floor.

"This feels right," I said, pushing myself off the floor.

"You're one big struggle recently, aren't you?"

"I'm glad it's bad enough for you to have noticed."

"Spill," LiQui said, *report* face on, before I could even buckle my seat belt.

So, on the way to Bookies—to talk to a million people about whatever—I told LiQui the whole story: about how I came to swear at whoever that teacher was, about my theory of the Lodenhauers buying Jack back into school, about the weirdness of it all. About how the Unlib was getting to be a demand on my time. About having Jack in freaking Queso and all the complications with Ashton and him and books.

Maybe that was the underlying current of what I'd felt since school started. Things seemed messy, muddled, and complex. It was like the feeling I had when I'd walk into my room and see the shirt hanging off a sconce on the wall or the expanding family of dirty coffee mugs on my nightstand, or when I'd find one running shoe under the bed and not have confidence that its brother was even in the room. I couldn't think or move without noticing more chaos. Once you realize something is messy, you can't go back. That's all it will ever be. That thing that's a mess.

It wasn't even expected mess either. Like, school had an expected mess. Intense homework. Football games. Hanging with friends. Those things were par for the course. That year, things were messy in ways I hadn't expected or even considered. The ways I had to sneak around and dole out books. The constant walking to my locker. The constant checking in and checking out. The pressure to do all this and still be a slayer student. The upcoming Founders Scholarship dinner and the corresponding scholarship hanging over my head. The growing knot I felt in my gut the more days that went by and the more books I checked out to people I didn't know. It was all like a layer of emotional fog.

Classes were starting to feel thick and clunky. I couldn't parse the information I was getting out as cleanly and quickly as I could before. Days were starting to blur together with white covers and locker trips. All this, and the end of the semester was so far away that people hadn't even begun to wish for it in normal conversation.

The words spilled out of my mouth, and the avalanche knocked some tears loose on the way down, so then I was crying in LiQui's car. I wasn't crying because of things I knew, but because of things I didn't.

I thought.

I didn't even know if the things I didn't know were the reason I was crying, which made me cry more. Suddenly, shutting down the Unlib, which had been a thought playing ding-dong-ditch with my brain, showed up on my front steps, not running away. It made me frustrated and confused because the Unlib wasn't something I'd ever had the intention of quitting. It was an "until graduation do us part" sort of project. I didn't have enough quotes yet to do anything with them, but . . . what had I thought those quotes would do? Had I even thought about what was going to happen? Would I just walk into Principal Walsh's office and hand him quotes and he'd go, *Oh yeah, you're right, Clara. Banned books are unbanned. Solid job. Ciao!*

Besides, since Scott had accused me of power-tripping, I couldn't shake the thought that I was a different version of Mr. Walsh. Both of us on our power trips. Each of us believing that we were in the right. Neither of us wavering. Locked in a battle. One I wanted to win. Desperately wanted to win. There was something off about everything I was doing, and I couldn't put my finger on it.

Was I turning books into weapons? Was winning enough? Was that all I wanted?

The feeling sank in my gut. No. Winning wasn't enough for the Unlib.

I needed a new reason to keep going.

A better reason. And it shouldn't have been that hard to find one. I believed in books, right? I was Clara Evans, book girl. Why wasn't it easier?

It was all still just as complex as when I'd started.

I took a breath.

And then another.

I closed my eyes.

Tried to shut my brain down for a millisecond.

Once I was able to do it for one, I shut it down for two.

Three.

Four.

Then I could breathe again.

Then I could see again.

I could feel the warmth of LiQui's hand on my knee, so I focused on that.

And I breathed.

And I focused on those two things until we got to Bookies.

## HONORS CENSORSHIP FOR THE ANGRY AND ILL-INFORMED

Everyone sat in the basement of Bookies, an old brick house converted to a bookstore by its owner, Ms. Lowe.

As soon as I saw bookshelves through the store windows, I felt lighter. Just thinking about the smell inside. Paper, compressed nature, and hands making words, a must of knowing and magic. Periods. Commas. Digressions. Analogies. The beauty of everyday thought turned poetry. It was all there, and I was hit with a little sliver of peace in the chaos of my brain.

"So, I'm going to be honest," I said to everyone. "I haven't had a chance to reread *Perks*. I mean, I could come up with stuff, and go off what I thought when I read it two years ago, but it's not fresh. I'm sorry. This is the first time since

Queso started that I haven't read the book in time, and I feel really bad about it."

The Queso regulars told me not to worry about it.

If only words worked on me at that moment.

"Thanks," I said, looking at Ms. Croft. "So, context for the normal Quesoians—this is one of my teachers, Ms. Croft. She was mysteriously fired, and she's here to tell my class why. Closure and all that. So, Ms. Croft, I know you came to talk, but I want to open it up to book stuff first? That way if any of the normals don't care to hear your story, they can leave. So. If anyone has anything to say about *Perks*, go ahead."

Silence. Not even Sean, who was my go-to guy to start us off, felt comfortable diving in.

The big crowd was too strange. It was fair—we'd been five to ten people since our inception, so to have a million people sitting around felt awkward. It felt more like a lecture and less like a discussion. It officially turned Queso into another messy thing. Normally, we showed up. Chatted. Quesoed. Had a blast. Went home. But then the star-star guys added themselves. And now talking about books was the opening act for LiQui's gossip table.

The ridiculousness of the night just added to the things that felt jumbled and shaky. Was there one steady thing? Somewhere?

"Well," I said, "all right, then. Normal Quesoians, sorry this has been a washout, but feel free to head out? Sorry. Next time, we need to pick our next six months of books. Be sure to think of ideas. Maybe we can come back to *Perks*."

As my book club transitioned into a strange second Honors Lit class, I went to the bathroom. Mostly to pee, but also to get away from everyone. To get away from Jack and the weight in his eyes that seemed heavier and heavier the more I was around him. To get away from Ashton and his paradigm-shifting niceness. To get away from LiQui and her all-knowing sage/lawyer brain, which had only gotten worse (better?) since school started. I needed a break.

I walked back downstairs—ready, I guessed, for the portion of the night where I would learn even more about LA politics. What fun.

"Ms. Croft," I said, "the table is proverbially yours."

She nodded and wasted no time taking it.

"First off, thanks for coming and letting me interrupt

your book club. When LiQuiana reached out to me to ask what happened, it really frustrated me she didn't know, especially since she's the student-body president. I felt like it was important for students to know what happened, even just my students, so coming here seemed like a natural option."

I nodded.

She continued. "I don't know how many of you know, but on the first day of school, administration released a banned-book list that included over fifty books. It was confidential. It didn't go out to students. I got angry for many reasons. Reasons I could talk about for a long time. But that's not the point. The point is, the ban, of course, affected classes. Specifically, my class material choices. So when administration asked me to redo my syllabus to take into account the new banned books, I did. Somewhat. I gave administration the old Honors Lit syllabus, but with changed titles. However, I secretly revamped the syllabus to something I thought of as Censorship for the Angry and Ill-Informed. I wanted to teach my Honors Lit class about censorship and its history. I wanted to push back by giving students the tools to understand the stakes of censorship and banning books.

"It wasn't what the school wanted—being a private school, they have the authority to ban what they want—but I was following their rules. I was teaching about court cases, not banned books. I was excited about it, and I got so distracted with coming up with the new program that I forgot to change the syllabus for my advanced English Comp class. I left in a banned book and turned in the syllabus as if it was complete. So, obviously, I was called into the principal's office for not adhering to the new school policy. He asked me to remove the book from my syllabus as I'd done with Honors Lit."

She paused. Took a breath. "As I stood there, witnessing this man ask me to not teach a book, it felt like simply being clever and subtle and teaching censorship court cases wasn't enough. I wasn't actually taking a stand. I was adjusting. So I said no, and they let me go for 'irreconcilable differences in school policy.' Clara," she said, turning to me. "After we talked that first day—remember? When we talked about *Don't Tread on Me*? I went home and finished it. I really believe *Don't Tread on Me* was the thing that gave me the conviction to say no to Dr. Walsh.

It's hard for me to divorce my reasoning from that book."

You would've thought Ms. Croft saying she was inspired by *Don't Tread on Me* would've been encouraging to me, but it made me more scared of the Unlib. She'd been inspired by the same book, for the same reasons, and she'd been fired.

The Founders Scholarship flashed into my mind. My ticket to college. The path of my future. I was a finalist. All the finalists got some money, but the winner got a full ride. To anywhere.

I hadn't thought about it until then, but me, LiQui, Vandy—that was all in danger. That was all in the cross-hairs. If I got caught, I'd be suspended. If I got suspended, I'd lose my chance at winning the Founders Scholarship.

What was I doing?

Did someone have a time car that could drive me back to the beginning of this semester?

Could I get a do-over?

"There's a banned-book list fifty books long?" a girl from Honors Lit asked. "How have we not heard about this?"

I pressed my lips together. I would not speak unless

it was a joke. I didn't trust myself, but I was fresh out of jokes.

Ms. Croft shifted in her seat. "We can bring this to court," she said. "In fact, I'm planning on it. I'm planning on going to the press in the next few days. I'm wondering if any of you would be interested in helping fight this?"

I froze. I didn't look up. I knew she expected me to say something. I was book girl. LitHouse, my Tiny Little Libraries, blah blah blah. If I didn't say yes, what was I? I just wanted the night to end. I was done. With the day. With all of it. I wanted to go home, deal with my parents, then slide into my bed and disappear into the land of my duvet cover.

The table was again silent.

"Well, think about it," Ms. Croft said. "LiQuiana has my email if you decide you want to be involved."

"Ms. Croft," LiQui said, "thank you so much for coming and giving us the deets. I'll connect with everyone in the morning and see if they want to jump into the fight."

Ms. Croft stood, and I could tell she wasn't going to let me leave without talking to me about my involvement in her crusade.

"Clara," she said, stepping toward me as everyone stood, grabbing their things.

"Look, Ms. Croft, I—"

"I'm surprised you don't want to help. Do you not want to? What would Levi and Joss do?"

I couldn't think. My mind felt like it was collapsing in on itself. Like the sheer weight of gray area combined with the unknown and how I was getting hangrier and hangrier was swallowing my ability to process.

"I've gotta go, Ms. Croft. We'll talk later."

And I walked away from her. Leaving her in the basement.

## AND THEN YOUR HERO HID IN THE AC NOOK OUTSIDE

*And I stared at the sky. The same sky my ancestors had looked at when freedom ran rampant like a river. Levi, inside, was bartering with money that wasn't ours for a book that could get us killed simply for referencing it.*

*In that combustion of time and consequence, I couldn't see the true colors of anything. Everything was history and monuments and the blur of power and death, and I wondered if all this was worth it. And I wondered if anyone else ever felt that. Lying in a foxhole. Shooting another man or woman. Was it worth it?*

*My head spun.*

*I found myself wanting bread, which, I felt, was just fine.*

*Despite what Levi said, there was a time and place for bread.*

—Lukas Gebhardt, *Don't Tread on Me*

* * *

I nearly ran out of Bookies, passing the shelves I'd been so happy to see just an hour earlier. I stood outside, in the shadow of the building, in a little nook where the AC unit sat, trying to get my brain to do something besides short-circuit under the weight of all the things I couldn't figure out.

A stream of people poured out through the door, and I watched as the parking lot emptied. I watched Ms. Croft leave, and I couldn't help but think that her small glance in my direction was because she smelled my guilt and confusion on the wind.

I stood, my back against Bookies. Looking up into the sky. I felt like Joss, when he had to step outside during a deal with one of their book dealers. He stepped out because he wondered if the fight was worth it; I'd stepped out because I wondered if I even knew what I was fighting for anymore.

The air and the hum of the AC settled around me and I closed my eyes. And for a minute there was nothing, and in that minute I tried to capture the nothing so I could shove it into my pocket and bring it out when I needed it.

"I read *Perks.* I'll read that other one next," a voice said. I opened my eyes, and Jack stood in front of me.

"Yeah? What did you think?" I asked, closing my eyes again. I wanted to focus on the nothing.

"It was beautiful."

The nothing faded. Replaced by my awe. I looked at him.

"*Perks* is the reason I came to your club," he said. "I heard that you were into it. I thought . . . I thought maybe we could talk about it. Maybe talking to you would be good."

"Talking to me? What do you mean?"

A loud "Yo!" split across the parking lot. LiQui. "Clara?"

"I'm here," I said, emerging from my nook of normalness. To my surprise, Ashton followed behind her. I looked at Jack. Any vulnerability he'd shown me retreated somewhere deep inside him, and the loss was incredibly disappointing.

"You okay?" Ashton asked me.

I let out a sarcastic snort. "I feel like I asked you that recently and didn't get an answer."

He gave me a sheepish grin.

"Have y'all met?" I said, motioning between him and LiQui.

Ashton shook his head, then held out his hand. "Hey, I'm a fan of your president work. You should for real run. Like, for the USA. I'd vote for you. I'll run your campaign."

LiQui's head cocked to the side. A smile, one part astonishment, two parts amused, turned her lips into a crescent O. She looked at me, and I gave her a knowing nod.

"Well, aren't you a glass of sweet tea?" she said.

"Oh God," Jack replied, and for a minute I thought he was mocking LiQui and I was about to pull out my verbal guns, but then he added, "Don't say shit like that about him. He doesn't need it."

"Look," Ashton said, "anyone who deals with LA administration without selling their soul and kissing ass is badass in my book."

LiQui fanned herself. "Keep going. Say more nice things."

Jack just stared at the ground.

"I would, but we've gotta go," Ashton said. "Clara, tonight was . . . weird. Really weird. Thanks."

"You're telling me." I looked at Jack. "Hey, I recommend

starting on *Catcher* after *Perks*. Holden and Charlie are super similar."

He nodded. Then they left.

LiQui turned to me as soon as they were out of earshot. "Come on. Let's split so we're not two punks standing in the dark."

I watched Jack walk away and wondered what I'd just seen from him. Wondered why he wanted to talk to me. Had that been his intention all along? If so, why had he been such a jerk about the club the first day he came? Why was he a jerk at all?

Where had the Jack Lodenhauer I'd just met come from?

**DON'T TREAD ON ME, CHAPTER 43: JOSS**

Levi was quiet, scribbling on a paper in the lamplight.

"What are we doing?" I said, tossing down my pencil. It echoed for eternity against the cave walls. "We're sitting here hiding when our world is still fighting. At least when we were soldiers, we were fighting."

Levi looked up. "Who says we're not fighting?"

I looked at him. "Are you fighting, right now?"

"Yes?" he said.

"Are you holding a gun?"

"No, but a gun is about as necessary to a fight as a hammer is to make soup."

"What are you doing, then?"

"I'm writing. I'm writing everything I've ever wanted to

*say, and I'm telling everyone everything they've ever done is just bread and circuses."*

*"What if people don't listen to anything but murder, crumbled cities, orphaned kids? Blood?"*

*"Then they'll listen to our stories."*

*"Stories have no power here, Levi. Stories aren't enough to end a war."*

*"Joss, what do you think started it?"*

## CAN THE DAY BE OVER ALREADY?

I could smell the parental disappointment as soon as I walked in. The house also smelled like put-away dinner, and we needed to have the *you snapped at a teacher, are you a serial killer now?* discussion before I could eat, so I just needed to accept being hangry for a bajillion more hours. I should've put my fist in the queso. The stupid choices I'd made.

Before I could even drop my bag, Mom emerged from the living room into the kitchen, Dad in tow. Mom had a *Star Wars* tee on the top half of her, and ripped jeans on the bottom half. A closer look revealed they were *my* ripped jeans. I didn't say anything. I figured most kids complained about their parents being uncool, and I knew for a fact that my mom wasn't even trying to be cool by wearing my ripped jeans and a *Star Wars* tee, which made her awesome. Really, though, if my wardrobe helped her be relevant to society, and made my friends jealous of having a mom who sometimes called my dad "bro," it was my duty to let it happen.

"Hey," she said, my dad following behind her.

"Hey," I said to both of them. "Long time no see, Dad."

That fall, my dad and I were running on schedules that had us going and leaving five minutes before the other. If I had some downtime at the house, he probably wouldn't be home, but without fail he'd get home either right before I left or a few minutes after. He was, and I say this without shame, a used-car salesman, so his hours were wonky. The good news was he was good at it. He had this unexplainable family-friendly look about him. Something about him—maybe it was his swoopy hair; name the last time you met a salesman with dark swoopy hair—said, *This man is freaking safe.*

"You must be her," he said, holding a hand out. "My name's Kevin Evans. I own the house you've been living in."

I shook his hand, happy he'd led with a joke. If he was

joking, then this wasn't going to kill me. Maybe I was reaping the benefits of having been too scared to be rebellious for most of my teenage career. "Pleased to meet you, sir. You own a fine establishment here. My only feedback is that the toilet paper could be softer."

He grabbed my backpack out of my hands and put it on the table, then wrapped me in his arms and pulled me into a hug. "I hear you've been up to things."

"Yep," I said. "Mostly just hanging out in dark alleys and taking selfies."

"What a daughter."

"What happened?" Mom asked, getting straight to it.

I pulled back from Dad's hug and then launched into the explanation I'd decided I felt comfortable giving. I told them about the banned-book list that no one knew about. About wanting to do something about it, but not that I *was* doing something about it. I told them about being caught with the copies of *The Chocolate War* from the library, except I blamed Mr. Caywell. I talked about figuring out the tricks of LA, about them saying they had a list but not actually having one. I told them about everything, excluding the Unlib.

I didn't tell them because I already knew it was dangerous, and I knew all the stuff that they'd say—I didn't need them telling me. I was already struggling with it. Feeling stupid for not knowing what to do. I didn't need them guilt-tripping up my way forward. I wanted whatever happened to be my choice.

"I don't know if that was smart, Clara." Mom's poetic cadence was gone, and she talked like a normal person. Always a bad sign.

"Jessica," Dad said, but she ignored him.

"What do you mean, specifically? There's a lot of things I told you," I asked.

"You have one year left and you're swearing at teachers? Playing with fire by pushing the limits with school rules?"

"Mom, I wasn't doing it to be rebellious. I was mad. Having a bad day. It's frustrating that my bad days are deep-seated issues with my character and every adult's bad days are just bad days. I don't get together with LiQui and plot how to cuss out every teacher."

"I understand about the teacher," she said calmly. "I guess I wonder about the pushing of the rules. What do you want from that?"

"I want to know what possible reasons these ridiculous policies are built on. Why it's considered a crime for me to read these books."

She nodded. "Those are good questions, but don't let fists replace the hard work of compassion and kindness."

"What are you trying to say, Mom? Just say it."

"Clara, easy," Dad said. "I know you're feeling attacked, but Mom is"—Mom shot Dad a glance of fire—"*we're* worried you'll jeopardize your chances for the Founders Scholarship. If you get in trouble at school, you could lose it."

"Well," Mom added, "Kevin, I'm not talking about the Founders Scholarship. That's not the point I'm trying to make right now. I'm saying I don't want Clara to turn into someone who's seeing demons behind every door. Waiting for something to protest. Living offended all the time. Looking for things to be mad at. That's more important to me than anything else."

"I mean, yes, fair, those are good things," Dad said. "Okay."

I rolled my eyes. "You say this like I get angry about things as much as I read books."

"I know you don't do that, Clara," Mom said. "I just want

you to think about it. That's all. I'm with you on the fact that those policies don't seem right. And I'm not against protesting or figuring out how to bring change through speaking out, but protests can't stop at a fist in the air. And they also can't stop with yelling. In our time, kindness is almost as revolutionary as protest, and I'd rather you be a rebel of kindness than a rebel of protest."

"Mom, I tried," I said, my voice sharpening in frustration. "I tried doing it the kind way. Writing a letter with my student-body president, inviting LA to talk to me about it. It was denied. What happens if all that's left is fighting?"

"Then fight, kindly."

I groaned. "What does that even mean?"

"A strong left hook to knock them out. An outstretched hand to help them up."

The room was silent, until finally Dad said, "The call was . . . a tad bit of a shock to us. The girl whose biggest rebellion has been staying up all night to read a book is also the girl who cussed at her teacher and tried to find a loophole in a rule."

"First of all, you know about the Evans Highlighter All-Nighter?"

My mom laughed. "Did you think it was pure magic that highlighters just appeared in your drawer when school started?"

I honestly considered what I had thought. "I think I thought they were the same ones from last time."

"Not possible. Highlighters disappear in this house." Mom glanced a loaded look at Dad, who I'd stolen my love of orange highlighters from. He used them to highlight sections in magazines, nonfiction books he picked up from bargain bins. Words he liked in crossword puzzles. He even wrote notes with them. That's where my love of them stopped. Reading a neon-yellow Post-it note written with orange highlighter stuck to a blue front door at 6:30 in the morning is a special kind of misery that I'd rather not perpetuate.

"My whole life has been a lie. How long have you known?"

"Always," Dad said. "Just like Snape."

I laughed and was about to respond, when Mom cut me off.

"We're getting off topic."

I sighed. "It's not a big deal, seriously. The teacher was

just a bad day. The loophole was just curiosity."

I guessed that was the problem with rarely pushing boundaries. When you did, regardless of what it was, suddenly you were reading *The Anarchist Cookbook*, getting a face tattoo, and smoking weed in the bathroom. It was frustrating beyond belief. No one was perfect, yet it seemed like I wasn't allowed to have imperfections or bad days. You were either an A student who never got in trouble or you were face-tattoo daughter. When I told my parents it wasn't a big deal, it wasn't that I wanted them to stop asking questions; I wanted them to let me fall in the middle of the two. To not worry that they'd somehow failed in their parenting.

"We're proud of you for all you've done in the last two years," Dad said. "We just didn't know you were having all of these problems with the school. You should've told us."

I shrugged. "Yeah, I guess I feel like there's not much you can do about it."

He shrugged. "Well, you can use us as sounding boards."

"We also want you to not live an offended and, therefore, a defensive and angry life," Mom added.

"Oh my God, Mom. Okay. I get it. I do. Stop acting like

I committed grand arson. There's a difference between being defensive and standing against something."

"First of all," Mom said, "standing *against* something is much less important than standing *for* something."

"Well, that's what I meant," I said, but I didn't know if it was. I guess I didn't know the difference between the two.

"Compassion and passion," Mom said, as if reading my thoughts. "You stand up because you believe, not because you want to win. I don't want you to add more hate to this world. We have enough. You can protest. You can question. But standing against someone or something can turn into hate without you even noticing. Hate is the worst place to start if you want to change something."

I couldn't argue with that.

I'd been against the star-stars since day one of high school, and, if I was honest with myself, I'd hated them. I'd hated every part of them without giving them the chance to be people. I'd written fiction that replaced who they actually were, and that was what defined them instead of the real them.

My own fiction.

I did hate.

Not only that.

If I'd started the Unlib wanting to win, then did I really believe in it?

God.

I couldn't think.

It all felt so heavy.

I put my head in my hands and cried.

Again.

# AN UNSEEN TEXT AT MIDNIGHT

**Unknown Number** [12:11 AM] Hey, this is Jack. I finished Catcher.

Can we talk tomorrow?

## RESPONDING TO AN UNSEEN TEXT IN THE MORNING

**Me** [5:58 AM] Hey, sorry I just woke up.

Awesome! I'll be at school early, in the library if you wanna talk about it.

Excited to hear what you thought.

## A SERIES OF SOME SORT OF EVENTS

*We cannot tell the precise moment when friendship is formed. As in filling a vessel drop by drop, there is at last a drop which makes it run over; so in a series of kindnesses there is at least one which makes the heart run over.*

—Ray Bradbury, *Fahrenheit 451*

My brain threatened not to exist, but at least the processing room looked as organized as it could get.

It looked *fine*.

Really freaking fine.

It'd be a good last project to leave Mr. Caywell with. I selfishly wanted my legacy as a library volunteer to be that whenever a student volunteer would do something,

Mr. Caywell would think, *Hmm, Clara could've done it better.*

I finally had a system down for going through the backlog of donation boxes: older than five years on one shelf, newer than five on another. "Banned" books stayed in their box. If they were ones the Unlib already had, then my plan was to bring them to a TLL. Not a lie. I was actually going to bring banned library books to my TLLs. If the banned books were books the Unlib needed extra copies of, a new pack of white construction paper sat in the drawer of an old brown desk against the far wall. The original plan was to make white covers right there. To manufacture the bane of LA's existence within its own walls. But I hadn't made a new white cover since I'd done the last three copies of *DTOM*, and it wasn't because the Unlib didn't need new white covers.

I pulled two books off a pile, both bannies. Both books that I, theoretically, wanted extra copies of for the Unlib: another copy of *Catcher in the Rye*, and a first copy of *The Adventures of Captain Underpants*, which, yes, was on the banned list. I tossed them onto the desk, where a few other books I "wanted" sat waiting for conversion.

I sighed and stared at the pile of unconverted books. "How is it even possible that you can stare back?" I asked them, and the door opened a millisecond after. I expected a gasping Mr. Caywell, spewing praise about how nice it looked, but instead it was Jack Lodenhauer. He looked . . . something. I don't know. It looked like his eyes went on and on and on. A never-ending spacelike infinity that seemed too vast for one person to handle.

He looked around the room. "Were you talking to some-one?"

"What? Me? Nope."

He shoved his hands in his pockets and looked at the floor. "Oh. I thought I heard you talking."

I waved him off, laughing awkwardly. "There's no one in here. I can't talk to no one. I mean, not that I've never talked to myself before, but today that is not what I was doing. I mean, I wasn't talking at all."

And then.

Jack Lodenhauer.

Started.

Crying.

I pushed myself off the desk and closed the door behind

him. The only thing I was thinking was, *Well, that's the last time I ever make that joke.* I didn't know if I should hug him or sit and wait. I'd hated Jack before the Unlib. Hated. Hated him so much that I would've never pictured a time or place where hugging was on the table for us, but that was shattered, because he leaned into me and cried into my shoulder. So, instead of being surprised and confused, I took it as the universe giving me the honor of that moment.

We stayed like that for a few minutes. Him crying. Me feeling the growing wet spot on my sleeve. Finally he backed away, and if he felt awkward for having had a breakdown in front of me, he didn't show it. Even if he did, I was fully prepared to tell him about my equally as impressive breakdown in LiQui's car on the way to Queso the night before. At least he retained the ability to breathe when he cried. Something I couldn't say for myself.

"I don't get it," he said, wiping the tears from his eyes.

"Get what? The book?"

"Why did Holden have to end up in a shitty mental hospital? Why couldn't he have turned out all right?"

"Well, I think he did? I mean, not as good as riding

into the sunset after winning the lottery, but, like, he was getting help, which was more of a start toward healing than he'd ever had before. He's finally investing in that part of himself. That might not be an ending of 'completely healed,' but I think that's more realistic, you know? We don't just get fixed."

"He ended up in a mental hospital. He's struggling with depression and he ends up in a mental hospital. So does Charlie from *Perks*."

"But there's so much more to these stories than that, though. I feel like that's a part that shouldn't be fixated on."

"There's only one time where Holden is happy. One time. When his little sister, Phoebe, is riding the carousel."

"Yeah, but it's because of her innocence. The whole book is about innocence. Keeping kids in kid land instead of growing up and dealing with all this crap." I waved my hands around the room. "But I feel like, in that moment, he realizes he has to grow into himself. He has to somehow grow up without growing old. He has to figure out how to have joy in the new Holden. Isn't that a good reminder? Like, to connect with him on that? To feel like you aren't alone?"

"Why did you give me this book?" he asked.

I cocked my head. I couldn't understand how he'd read the same book I had. How could he be so frustrated with it? How could it spur me to change the world, to grow up well, yet make him nearly inconsolable? For me it was like: be kind and listen to everyone. I walked away thinking, *People breathe. People eat. People carry heavy things. You've got a pulse; you've got a problem.* Because it made me think about the world as a place where everyone was sort of ambling around in their own weakness. Scared. Anxious. It made everything feel less scary knowing Holden was there too.

"Childhood innocence can't stay forever, and I don't think it should," I said. "All these people act like it's the highest form of happiness, but it's all based on ignorance. Kids are happy because they're ignorant of the world, which is good. For kids. But for us? Isn't it so much more powerful to choose happiness knowing what the world truly is? To fight for it? To make our joy in the face of it all? I thought, maybe, you'd sort of wind up there too."

Jack leaned against the wall. Eyes closed. Silent, yet it was clear he wanted to say something and couldn't find the strength to do it. It was the same face he'd had when we talked in the AC nook, and being in the light let me see it.

"What?" I said. "Just say what you need to. I won't get mad."

He shook his head. "I can't."

I raised an eyebrow. "Why not?"

"Because I live in the South. Because of who I am. I'm not supposed to say it."

"Jack, I'm not sure what you're trying to say. Last time I checked, people in the South were allowed to not like *Catcher in the Rye*. It's okay if you want to slam it. We have different tast—"

"I'm gay. The only people who know are Ashton and Resi. You think Holden makes me feel like I belong? Or Charlie? They make me feel screwed. Like, he isn't even gay. He doesn't even have a family who's literally threatened to make him live on the street. He's just a kid who's depressed. Phoebe isn't giving him the cold shoulder every time he comes home. I want that childhood innocence. I don't even want to be the catcher in the rye. I want to be the one caught. I want someone else to be there. But no one is. So why would you think I'd prefer being reminded of the world and how much it hates me over living in ignorance?"

I looked at him. Tears began to stream silently down his face again. I didn't know what to say. I had nothing.

I'd always assumed that people who didn't experience a book the same way as I did weren't looking at it right. They missed the point. They misunderstood it. But, suddenly, there was context to consider. Was I privileged enough to be able to love books in which hurt flowed abundantly without feeling more hopelessness? Was it privilege, or did it change from person to person? Or was it both? But I had friends who loved this book. Friends who hurt deeply but connected in the same way I had. Quesoian Sean was one of them. He was reading *Perks* when his mother died of cancer and it made the book even more special to him.

"I'm . . . I'm really sorry, Jack. I didn't know."

"Yeah, well. So am I. No one knows. No one will know. You can't tell anyone. If word gets out about me, my parents will completely disown me. They'll talk to all their friends and I won't be able to get a job. I won't be able to find a place to live. This is me."

"Don't worry. I won't tell anyone. Is there any way I can help? Will it be different once you go to college? You're a Founders Scholarship finalist, right? If you win that then you can go anywhere you want."

I said it like there was a chance he couldn't go anywhere he wanted, but we both knew that was a lie. He didn't need the Founders Scholarship for the money, but I didn't know what else to say.

He shook his head. Then shrugged. "I don't know. See, if I leave . . . if I leave and live like the real me? I'm out of the family. The money. The connections. It's all gone."

I looked at the ground. I needed to say something. Anything. A quote? Something to make it better. But I couldn't. I had no idea what would help. My go-to was to give the conflicted a book, but I'd already given the conflicted a book—four, actually—and there he was. Hurting even more because of those books.

"It doesn't help that this school hates me too. Everyone hates me."

"I don't hate you," I said.

"Of course you do. The way you looked at me that first night I came to your club thing? Of course you hate me. *I* hate me."

"Okay . . . okay. Yes. I did. *Did*. Hate you. But it's just because I didn't know you."

"What's to love now that you 'know' me? I'm a gay Holden. Bitching about everything with the added bonus of bearing the scarlet letter of the conservative South."

"Jack . . ."

"Emerson is a freshman here. Have you seen him talk to me at all?"

I hadn't. In fact, it was only then that I realized: Emerson didn't sit at the star-star table. Emerson, his younger brother, was pretending that Jack didn't even exist.

"Ashton and Resi are the only friends who have never hated me. And I'm sure they do by now anyway."

He went silent.

"Do you like him?" I asked. "Ashton?"

He shook his head. "No."

"Well . . . at least there's that."

Jack stared at me for a second, then laughed. "Yeah. At least."

I looked him in the eyes. "How can I help you?"

He shrugged. "I don't know. I don't even know how to help me."

"I think you're stronger than you think."

"I'm not. I got that DUI on purpose. I wanted to get suspended from this hellhole. To finish out my senior year in a place that didn't whisper my name in every corner. But my mom likes that. She thinks it keeps me straight. Accountable. So she bought me back in. Back into the place that watches me for her."

"So your family knows?"

He nodded. "Yeah. They know. I came out to them last year. Hence why Emerson doesn't talk to me."

More silence.

"Not going to lie." I paused. "Your mom sounds downright horrible."

He laughed again, but didn't say anything.

"Hey, I have a new book for you. This one will cheer you up. I promise. Wait here," I said, walking over to the desk. I pulled two sheets of white construction paper out of the drawer, and in a few minutes I'd wrapped the status-pending copy of *The Adventures of Captain Underpants*, added it to my app, and checked it out to Jack using his old info. I handed it to him. He took it and looked it over.

"*Captain Underpants,*" he said flatly.

"It's banned, believe it or not."

"I believe it. Promise you won't tell anyone."

"I promise."

More silence.

"Can I ask you a question?" I said.

He nodded.

"You don't know me. Why did you tell me?"

*"Perks,"* he said, simply. "I checked it out a year ago, back when it wasn't banned, and Mr. Caywell said, 'Oh, this is one of Clara's favorite books.' I figured if you loved that book, then maybe you'd understand. Maybe you'd care."

A tear formed at the corner of my eye. I brushed it away as it came. "But why tell me at all?"

"Because I feel so alone I just want to not be here. Anyway, it's one of the reasons I dragged Ashton to your book club. I wanted to see . . . I wanted to find a place I could be understood."

"So when I snapped at you, I confirmed that even the people you thought might understand, wouldn't."

He shrugged. "We don't need to get into it."

"But it's true."

"You apologized."

"That doesn't matter—I was still a jerk to you for no reason."

"Yeah, well, same. I do the same thing to everyone else. It's not like we're that different."

"So . . . that's it?"

"What?"

"We accept the hate we're given because everyone hates someone?"

"Well, yeah, everyone hates," he said. "It's just a matter of if it's someone else or yourself."

"That doesn't make it better, Jack. Don't accept that."

"I'm not accepting it!" he yelled. "It's just really damn ridiculous to think we don't or won't hate anyone. It's better to learn how to see it in ourselves—then we'll *know* when we hate, and knowing will make it easier to stop."

I sighed. He had a point.

"Who do you hate?" I asked, leaning against the wall next to him.

"Everyone. And myself."

"So, if you know that, then can you stop?"

He shook his head. "No. I don't know why I hate. I just

know I do. How can you stop what you don't know?"

"Maybe it's less hate and more anger."

He shrugged. "I'm not sure what the difference is."

I didn't know either, I guessed.

"Jack." I looked up at him. "You are handcrafted and artisan-made. You're batch one of one, and I wish I could take all that . . . shit from your life, your mom, your family and toss it in the trash. I don't really know what else to say outside of I'm here and you don't have to be alone."

He nodded. A simple, clean, easy, *Sure* kind of nod, and it hit me that maybe he'd heard all of this and that it didn't help.

Maybe, after all the words I'd read in my life, I was finally fresh out.

## RUNNERS, JUMPERS, RACERS, TINKERERS, GRABBERS, SNATCHERS, FLIERS, SWIMMERS

I needed either a nap or a bucket of fried chicken.

School was over. I shoved my locker shut, and then tapped in the data for the last check-in of the day. I'd had seven people check in books at lunch, and I hadn't had time to update the app. I hadn't even had time to consider the conversation I'd had with Jack that morning, even though it pressed on me with every millisecond that passed by.

That day, in order to get every book checked out, I stayed a little after school. Once I finished, I texted LiQui. I hadn't even gotten a chance to step foot into the cafeteria. It had been straight books through lunch. The only food I'd had was a cookie LiQui shoved through my locker slot. I'd told her we needed to hang out that night and that

I needed chicken—not cheese for once (strange days)—
ASAP.

On my way out of the school, I swung by the library to
grab the history homework I'd left in the processing room,
which, now that it was clean, had become more than a
resting place for donated books, doubling as a dumping
place for all my stuff.

I walked into the library, coming in on the side closest
to the shelves and out of sight of the desk. Before I popped
into view, I heard Mr. Walsh. I stopped and disappeared
behind a bookshelf, not wanting to touch that mess.

I looked through the stacks. There he was. The dictator
of LA. Back to me. Arms crossed. Looking like a dictator.
The polished buckle of his tight gray suit vest glinting the
light onto the wall.

"There's an ex–staff member going to the press about
the prohibited-media list," Mr. Walsh said. His voice sounded
strained and harried. Ex–staff member. Press. Ms. Croft
must've struck. "I have a little pull with the people at the
*Times Free Press*—a Lupton alum is one of the editors
there—but if there is an article, and it is printed . . . well.
I need your word, your absolute collaboration on dealing

with this. We'll have to handle the press with the most precious of care. We are in the midst of the SPA agreements, and we don't need any negative press. Not only that, but we don't need a hubbub about books that simply don't matter."

"Dr. Walsh, you know where I stand on this. I'm not going to lie to kids and tell them, 'Sorry, we don't have that one,' when it's very obviously banned. The library is not a place for those sorts of things."

"I disagree, Mr. Caywell. Change the subject. Offer a different book that is similar. Tell them you don't have the one they are asking for, but that they can request it. Many options. You need to decide, because she's . . . they are going to the papers in the next few days, and I need you on my team."

Mr. Caywell sighed. "I'm going to respectfully decline. The students knew administration got rid of *The Hunger Games* when it was banned, and being dodgy only made things worse. They're smarter than you're giving them credit for. I'll simply tell them they've been removed from circulation until further notice."

"You will do exactly what I ask, and that is not what I am asking."

Mr. Caywell smiled, but it was a smile that meant everything smiles didn't mean. "I will not lie on behalf of the administration to every student who walks into my library and asks for a banned book. Especially about a policy I do not find fair, do not agree with, and was not consulted or warned about."

Mr. Walsh nodded. His hands pressed into his sides. "I hear you, Mr. Caywell. I hear you. And do call them 'prohibited media.' 'Banned book' is way too aggressive. Anyway, perhaps a few mandatory days off would help you remember that you were employed to serve the school and its students. We can call it a 'short sabbatical for personal reasons.' At least until this blows over."

Holy semicolon.

No way.

What?

Mr. Caywell laughed. "You're serious?"

"Absolutely. I've been charged with making this school the best it can be, and it, and a deal I've fought for since I began here hangs in the balance. If we don't nip this in the bud right now, we will see a heap of trouble land on our welcome mat. I respect that you do not agree, and

I respect your work. So, if you do not want to comply in this simple matter, then, for the sake of this school, that is what I must do. You must hear my sincerity. You've been with Lupton for eight years. You're a great librarian. The students love you. We disagree here, and I think this is a good way to meet in the middle."

Mr. Caywell stared at him. Probably thinking the same thing I was thinking. Did Mr. Walsh really think that having the library closed during negative press about banned books was the answer?

"You know what, Dr. Walsh? That sounds great. I'm going to go visit my mom."

Mr. Walsh actually smiled, but not in a *Victory!* way. He smiled like he thought he'd actually given Mr. Caywell something he deserved. Like he really did believe he was doing the right thing.

Mr. Walsh put his hand on Mr. Caywell's shoulder. "Good. It'll be paid time off, of course. Least I can do."

Mr. Caywell grabbed a shoulder bag off the floor and started packing his things. "Generous of you," he said drily.

"Thank you for understanding, Mr. Caywell. Now I'm off. Have to assure the powers that be that all has been taken care of. Ha! Cheers! If all goes well and stays quiet, we'll see you back here next Monday."

"Sounds great."

Mr. Walsh swiveled on his heel like he'd had one of the best conversations in his life. A pep in his step only matched by a kid who got a red Mustang for their sixteenth birthday. He shoved his hands in his pants pockets and started to whistle. I waited for the whistling to fade down the hallway before emerging.

Mr. Caywell put a finger on the library light switches as I came into plain view. He nodded like he'd expected me.

"Of course you're here. You smelled blood."

"You're just going to shut down the library?" I said. "Like, LA is not going to have a library?"

"Do you really think that's going to go unnoticed?"

I shook my head. "No, I don't."

"Don't you think that the library being closed is a better nail in the coffin than it being open? He's digging his own grave. This is the move I've wanted from him since I started working here. Something so rash and political that he'd miss the obvious. Me leaving is for all the books he's ever banned."

It hit me that, for him, this was all so clear. He'd put

in his time dealing with the crazy, and now suddenly he
had the chance to stand for what he believed. All along,
I'd thought Ms. Croft had been the one fighting. The one
actually doing something. But this had been calculated.
He wasn't rioting in the streets. He'd infiltrated. Waited.
Now he was striking. Brilliant.

It was strange, because the way he talked about leaving
almost felt like he was doing it out of revenge. *Me leaving
is for all the books he's ever banned.* What I didn't understand was that if he was acting out of revenge, then where
was the line? *Was* there one? Was Ms. Croft acting out of
revenge or belief? Could you act out of both? Where on
that line did it turn wrong? Why was everything always
so confusing?

He turned off the library lights while I ran back to the
processing room and grabbed my stuff. I followed him outside and watched him pull down two large security grilles
that spanned the length of both openings to the library,
and lock them.

When he finished, he turned to me and said, "Dr. Walsh
and I only agree on one thing right now: I can best serve
this school by not being here." He held out his hand to the

library. "I expect something from you, Clara. I don't know what it is or what it should be. But this closed library is an impulsive gift from Principal Walsh. Don't waste it."

The weight of his "don't waste it" slipped onto the weight of Ms. Croft's "why don't you help me?" from the previous night's Queso.

"Tell your mom I said hi," I said flatly as Mr. Caywell walked away.

His laugh echoed through the hallway. "I'll do that. Maybe I'll even bring you some of her famous chocolate-chip banana muffins."

I stared through the slats of the security grille. I was so done with the weight. The whole thing was getting out of hand. If Mr. Walsh would go so far as to shut down the library to avoid problems, he was smoking a special kind of power trip. I couldn't do anything about that. I couldn't risk everything my senior year. Levi and Joss were living in a war zone; it was death on all sides for them. For me, it was my future.

Could I believe in books and quit the Unlib? Did believing in something have to mean ultimate sacrifice? Was there ever a time where not sacrificing was better for the greater good? If I kept the Unlib going, I could jeopardize the Founders Scholarship. I could miss out on Vanderbilt with LiQui. I could completely miss out on having the money to even go to college. If I went to college, would that put me in a better place to fight? To do more good?

What if there wasn't a next time?

What if there was a next time and I said the same thing, "next time"?

But . . . regardless of next time, regardless of any of these questions, the Unlib wasn't just some fanciful plot in some book. It wasn't just something I'd done to prove Mr. Walsh wrong. I didn't start it because of my belief in books. It was my own power trip. Using books as weapons to win a war instead of collecting books to bring unity. I wasn't Levi or Joss. I was another Mr. Walsh, fighting a fight, forcing my own opinions about books and which ones were the best on everyone else. It wasn't going to work.

I had to stop.

I needed to stop.

I took a breath. Felt the worry of all the *Should I? Should I not?* lift off my chest. I felt free. I'd made a choice. Finally.

The real library was closed. I couldn't quit now. I'd fill in for Mr. Caywell. I'd be the library until he came back. When the real library opened again, I'd be done. I'd really move the white covers out of school and into my Tiny Little Libraries, and I'd focus on graduating and getting out of LA. That was my long-term plan, and I felt good about it. I also felt good about my short-term plan: getting fried chicken for dinner.

## BOOK HONEY

*I feel sorry for anyone who is in a place where he feels strange and stupid.*

—Lois Lowry, *The Giver*

I held a giant John Deere mug filled with mango nectar and stared at my personal copy of *Don't Tread on Me*. Wanting so badly to read it again, but instead thinking about Jack. Thinking about our conversation. About how I'd hated him for so long and hadn't even noticed that I hated him and how that had added to his hurt, even though we didn't know each other. I wondered what I could do to help him. Or, at the very least, what book would actually give him some hope. All of this, but I also wondered if I dared to read *DTOM* again. The book had already shifted fault lines in my life in ways I couldn't even process. Did I want to refamiliarize myself with it? Luckily, I was handed a distraction from the book gods when my dad knocked on my door.

"Yeah?"

He opened it. "I love knocking on your door, because that means you're actually home."

I laughed. "Can't have a burgeoning nonprofit career, good grades, friends, and a home life."

"Why do you think I became a car salesman?"

"The shame?"

"So I can have it all, baby!" he said.

I laughed.

"Anyway," he said, "the reason I'm knocking is that there's a LiQui at the door downstairs."

I finally turned to face him. "Did you let her in?"

"She didn't want to come in. Y'all are going somewhere for dinner?"

I stood up. "Fried chicken. It's been calling to me all day."

Dad nodded. "I understand. That happens to me with pizza."

"Oh. Pizza. That sounds good too."

"Sorry. I didn't mean to come between you and fried chicken."

I sighed and rolled out of bed. "Why do you hate me?"

He gave me a big hug. "Tell chicken I said hi."

"I'll tell chicken that my dad doesn't approve of our relationship and that he'd rather I date pizza."

Dad grimaced. "How do you think chicken will take it?"

I shook my head. "Not well."

"It's for the best. Bye."

"Time heals all wounds. Bye."

I ran downstairs, passed Mom, and slipped out the front door. LiQui sat on my front stairs.

"Hi?" I asked, sitting down, and she instantly collapsed into my arms and shook with tears for at least five minutes. Did I put off pheromones that said *cry on me*? What was happening?

Finally, she said, "Sorry, you were probably reading some amazing book that'd make you wanna do something crazy and brave while I sat here being a pushover."

I didn't know what was happening that made her think she was a pushover, or how to answer. Not because I didn't want to, but mostly because when LiQui spilled, you let her spill.

"I'm mad at Lukas," she said. "Raging. It doesn't matter that he's sexy."

"Lukas?" I asked, confused. "Oh, you mean, like, *my* Lukas? What did he do?"

She nodded. "Not *Don't Tread on Me*—that one was just all right."

"I'll forgive you for that."

"I'm talking *A House of Wooden Windows*."

"Oh," I said. "Yeah, that one punches too."

She sat down, brushing tears out of her eyes. "I think I want to be president."

"Not to be insensitive, but, like, aren't you that . . . already?"

"No, like of the USA."

"Oh, that's not a minor jump. Is this because of what Ashton said?"

She glared at me. "I'd settle for senator. It's just . . . Not that you can't change stuff with business-degree cash, but I want to change stuff like Lila Stavey. I want to fight with craft like Levi and Joss. I want to be a lawyer. Then

I want to be a senator. Then president. I was chill with business degree–ing it, seriously, but since this whole thing with, like, researching students' rights and private-school contract law, digging into how the administration works and all the other junk I've been doing because of your book thing, not to mention watching you do your own shit, then reading *Wooden Windows*, it feels disingenuous to me to go get a business degree when I feel that civic leadership and doing grassroots change is in me bone deep. I don't know. Maybe it's crazy."

She trailed off.

"Qui, that's . . . incredible. Like, purely incredible." I nodded. "I don't think you're crazy. I see it in you too. I think you'd be amazing."

She smiled and brushed a tear out of her eye. "I see why you like your Book Honey so much; dude is a heavy hitter."

"So you *did* like *Don't Tread on Me*."

"I'm just saying, *Wooden Windows* is much better."

"So . . ."

"So. I don't know what to do. Should I blow the family to pieces with the new plan? If the grandrents drop, my mom and dad will be furious. Then I'll probably end up going to community college while you go to Vandy."

I looked at her. "I'm sure if you told your grandparents you wanted to be president of the US, they'd forgive you for not getting a business degree?"

"You don't know my grandparents."

"Yeah, you're right. What do your parents say?"

"'They're paying; do what your grandparents say.'" She sighed. "Anyway, let's go get fried chicken. I figured these tears were your fault and driving emotionally impaired would've gotten us into a ditch, so I needed to spill them here."

"Technically, they are Lukas's fault. He wrote the book that started the Unlib."

"Nah, he didn't make me read *House of Wooden Windows*."

"I didn't either." I held up a finger. "I shoved *Don't Tread on Me* in your hands. Not *House*."

"Oh, then, I guess technically these tears are the Mav's fault."

"What else is new?"

"Right?" She sighed. "Oh, he asked me on a date, FYI."

"Who did?" I asked.

"The Mav—aren't you paying attention to all my conversations happening at once?"

I found myself stunned for the second time. "Uhhhh. I thought y'all were, I quote, 'done with a capital *F* for forever.'"

"He read *Eleanor and Park* and apparently realized that Park was everything he wanted to be as a boyfriend and here we are."

"So . . ."

"President takes precedence."

I laughed. "Like I always say, department of state before a mate."

She snorted, then wiped another tear off her cheek.

"Do you feel good about that? Saying no to him, I mean?"

"Yeah. He's going to go off to some school and play football and, even if we stuck around each other, we're nowhere near the same gravity. But it's still funny to think he got all these grand romantic ideas from a book."

"Well, the Mav aside, I'm sorry about the grandparents, LiQui. That's a really hard thing."

"I know," she said as she leaned into me. "Why is it

that knowing who you are just makes things harder sometimes?"

I immediately thought of Jack. I thought of me. I
thought of everyone.

"The same reason knowing what you believe is so confusing to figure out."

"What reason is that?"

"Fear, I guess."

A few seconds of silence passed between us.

I stood and pulled LiQui up. "So, how would you feel
about getting pizza instead?"

LiQui scoffed as if she was offended I was considering
different dinner plans, but then she tilted her head in consideration. After a beat, she looked at me with a face that
said, *Why does every decision have to be so hard?*

I nodded. "Yeah. Tell me about it. Let's just start driving and see what happens."

## THE LIBRARIAN IS HANGING OUT WITH HIS MOM

Three strange things:

My body was trained to wake up early. The library was closed. Our librarian was hanging out with his mom.

These things created a problem: I woke up early but had nowhere to go. So I made a new tradition. I answered some LitHouse emails, then checked a few of my TLLs, making sure they were stocked. Then, right before getting on the highway, I stopped at a gas station to see if the newspaper had any story about Lupton, but there wasn't a single mention of LA.

Even after all that, I still had some time to kill, so I decided to drive through downtown Chattanooga instead of taking the highway. Driving downtown was longer

because of the sheer amount of stoplights between my
house and LA.

The new route brought me past the courthouse, and
under the Art District, home of the Hunter Museum of
Art, the museum where, on one school trip, LiQui put her
glasses on the floor and we watched museumgoers stare
at them like they were an art installation. There were four
bridges that crossed over the Tennessee River: Highway
27 (my normal route), the Market Street Bridge (the one
I took that day), the Veterans Memorial Bridge, and the
Walnut Street Bridge. The Walnut Street Bridge wasn't
for cars, though; it was one of the world's longest pedes-
trian bridges.

Sometimes, LiQui and I would walk the Walnut Street
Bridge after school if we didn't feel like heading home
immediately. It was one of my favorite places in Chattanooga. You got to stand over the river and look out on its
murky and ancient currents. On days where there weren't
clouds, I liked to believe that the bridge's blue trusses
were an integral part of the Earth's atmosphere, and if it
weren't for Chattanooga, the sky would cave in.

Finally, I pulled into Lupton like a normal student,

grabbing one of the last spots in the senior parking lot. I walked around the roundabout and into Lupton Hall, and as soon as I walked inside, I felt the whispers about the library before I even got to class.

Oh.

And Jack wasn't in class, again.

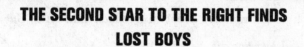

## THE SECOND STAR TO THE RIGHT FINDS LOST BOYS

One look at our lunch table proved that the world was tilting in ways incomprehensible.

Ashton sat in the open spot next to where I usually sat. Luckily, everyone was too busy whispering about the closing down of the library to whisper about the new occupant of our table. It was strange that the thing that made people forget about table rules was not having a library.

"Hey," I said to Ashton. "Welcome to the second star to the right."

He looked at me, confused, but then glanced up, spent a moment doing locational math. Then, glancing at the sun painting above our heads, he chuckled. "Why haven't I sat here before today?"

LiQui shrugged. "We've been here all along, bro."

"What? I thought it was perfect over there," Scott added, the first thing out of his mouth.

I had to promptly shoot him a look that said, *Cut the rich-kid jokes or die.*

Scott grimaced. "Sorry. Didn't mean to put you in a pigeonhole."

"Scott," LiQui corrected. "It's 'I didn't mean to pigeon-hole you.'"

"Either way, aren't you in a pigeonhole?" Scott asked.

"Sooo," I said, looking back at Ashton. I wanted to talk to him about Jack. About Jack's family. How miserable Jack seemed to be. To make a plan on how to help him. But the cafeteria table wasn't the place. "What's up? Jack was back and then he wasn't."

He shrugged, not sure if he wanted to share, but he must've felt safe enough to venture out a little bit, which made me feel proud. We were a safe space. "Everyone's mad at someone. I'm mad at Jack. Jack is mad at Resi. Resi is mad at me for being mad at Jack. It's a whole thing. Anyway, I need to talk to you, Queen Li."

I wondered if Ashton knew I knew about Jack. He

hadn't given me any looks that said, *Yo, you know now*, so I assumed he didn't.

LiQui fanned herself. "Go on."

"So you know the GSA?"

LiQui cocked her head. "Gay-Straight Alliance? Yeah?"

"You know that we haven't gotten club funding since we've been official? Two years?"

LiQui's mouth dropped. "Shut up. That *cannot* be true. No."

"Well, I read *DTOM* last night, and because of it, I want to change everything I hate, so this morning I stopped by Principal Walsh's office three times to ask about getting funding."

"That book, man," LiQui said. "Dangerous."

I smiled at the fact that I wasn't the one who'd said it. "Wait, so you've been running the GSA? Why haven't you brought up funding until now?"

Ashton laughed. "It's Lupton, man! They do this kind of thing and there's nothing we can do. I see behind the scenes of all the money. Y'all really don't know how little power we have. You know the idiom 'money talks'? Well, here, money teaches. Money makes the rules. Money erases public records. Money buys out suspensions."

LiQui shrugged. "For real. I knew that, sort of, being in StuCab, but I didn't know it was that bad until this year."

"The worst," he said, stabbing a fork into a sad-looking Caesar salad.

"So . . . why now, then?" I asked. "Why fight it now? Why fight it when you know it's not going to do anything? Asking for a friend."

LiQui snorted.

"Because . . ."

I knew why. Because it was the only way he felt like he could fight for Jack. Jack. A kid whose family held the biggest legacy at LA. A legacy that wouldn't fund a club that would support their own son. I could see the weight in Ashton's eyes so much clearer now. He was no longer the best bro of the biggest rich jerk on the planet. He wasn't a star-star anymore. He was a fiercely loyal friend who didn't know how to help.

"So? What happened? Did you talk to Mr. Walsh?"

"He was never there," Ashton said. "Always gone."

"I think he's got a second office somewhere," LiQui said.

"Does anyone know if he owns a Fitbit?" I asked.

"What they're doing has to be against bylaws some-where, right? I want to have an event for once."

LiQui hung her head. "After all the research I've done, no. We're a private school. They can discriminate any way they want."

Ashton sighed. "God, why have I spent three years here?"

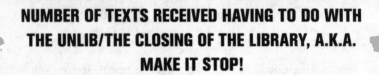

## NUMBER OF TEXTS RECEIVED HAVING TO DO WITH THE UNLIB/THE CLOSING OF THE LIBRARY, A.K.A. MAKE IT STOP!

At lunch: 5

After lunch: 24

After calculus: 35

As I was doling out white covers after school: 41

When I got home from school: 56

Before I left for the football game: 67

# A FANCY EMAIL FOR CLARA

Part A: The Email

To: clara.evans@luptonacademy.edu

From: shellibrown@foundersfoundation.org

Subject: Founders Scholarship Dinner Final Details!

Ms. Evans,

On behalf of everyone here at the Founders Foundation, I again want to congratulate you on being a Founders Scholarship finalist. This email is a friendly reminder that the Founders Scholarship Dinner is right around the corner! We're all excited to hear the finalists' speeches, and thank you in advance for all the work you've done preparing for

this event. Please see below for all the details and information you'll need for next Saturday.

Where: Hunter Museum of American Art

When: 6:45 p.m.

Attire: Formal

Table number: 6. Your table's guest of distinction will be
Janet Lodenhauer, founder of the Chattanooga Educators'
Commission for Change. Please come prepared with a few
questions.

Dinner: After a brief time of hors d'oeuvres, dinner will be
served at 7:15. If you or anyone in your party have any food
allergies that need to be taken into consideration, please
respond to this email ASAP.

If you have any questions, please feel free to ask!

Thank you,

Shelli Brown

Chair of the Founders Foundation


Part B: My Subsequent Reaction

Shit.

I forgot. I forgot. I forgot. I forgot. I forgot. I forgot. I
forgot. I forgot. I forgot. I forgot. I forgot. I forgot. I forgot. I

forgot. I forgot. I forgot. I forgot. I forgot. I forgot. I forgot. I forgot. I forgot. I forgot. I forgot. I forgot. I forgot. I forgot. I forgot. I forgot. I forgot. I forgot. I forgot. I forgot. I forgot. I forgot. I forgot. I forgot. I forgot. I forgot. I forgot. I forgot. I forgot. I forgot. I forgot. I forgot. I forgot. I forgot. I forgot. I forgot. I forgot. I forgot. I forgot. I forgot. I forgot. I forgot.

I forgot about the speech.

I have to prepare something in a week. I need clothes. I need to figure out if my parents can even go. I was going to ask Lukas, but it's too late notice for him. I need to prepare something in three days.

## FOUR ON A BLEACHER

*The library accumulated slowly. Like a steady snow. I thought it beau-*
*tiful. How fitting was it that the very things that worked their truth in*
*us over time also took the time to work on themselves.*

—Lukas Gebhardt, *Don't Tread on Me*

It was Friday, and for the first time in all my years of high
school, I sat with three people at a football game. LiQui,
Jack—who hadn't been in class, or at school for that matter, today, but I wasn't going to ask—and Ashton.

I hadn't realized how many people Ashton actually
talked to at this school. I mean, he was nonstop back and
forth with almost everyone. He was like a one-man PR
event, and it was strange for me to watch because I had

this very clear picture in my mind of him literally not talking to anyone but the star-stars. I'd had it for years. How had I missed this about him? How had I not seen that Jack was a hurting soul, a product of being told to change, that he wasn't good enough, and that he had no problems because he was rich?

Why had I thought that someone couldn't hurt? Hurt was rainwater. Falling and dripping everywhere. There wasn't a single place it didn't douse, so why was it that it was acceptable to write off one person's hurt if we considered it less than? It was as if we believed there was a universal standard for what the context of hurt needed to be before we could be empathetic.

As I thought of all this, I stared at Ashton and watched him interact with Jack, in awe of him . . . my friend. Two friends, who both, to me, felt like brand-new people who had just joined LA. LiQui saw my staring. Then nudged me with her leg and leaned over and whispered, "You for real right now?"

I turned. "What? Oh, Ashton? No. I'm just . . . no. Isn't it crazy what we think we know?"

LiQui looked unimpressed. "Mm-hmm. Right."

"Seriously! Like how did we end up here? With Jack Lodey and Ashton Bricks on our bleacher?"

LiQui shrugged. "I don't know, but . . . it's fun."

I stood as someone on the field caught a ball and did a thing. "I'm going to go get some snackies. I'll be right back."

Another thing I noticed: if it wasn't someone talking to Ashton, it was someone talking to me about the library, which, at that moment anyway, I didn't want anything to do with. For a while I answered honestly, but I got so sick of being poked at that my snark level grew with every second.

At the start of the game:

Them: "Do you know why it's closed?"

Me: "Nope. Completely clueless."

Them: "Your library is going to stay open, right?"

Me: "Until the library comes back."

An hour later:

Them: "Why is the library closed?"

Me: "The books are infested with commas."

Two hours later:

Them: "Why is the library closed?"

Me: "No one knows how to turn on the lights."

By the end of the third quarter:

Them: "Why is the library closed?"

Me: "Someone dropped a hamburger from the cafeteria by the circulation desk and it linked our world to a parallel universe, so now there's this gaping hole in the floor that you can look in and see how you're faring in an alternate reality. I mean, if you're not already dead. Anyway, we're waiting for the maintenance team to fix it. Can't have students freaking out about their mortality when Lupton's first principle is 'focus,' you know?"

With every question asked of me, I felt the pressure of being LA's sole ambassador of literature stack like bricks on my shoulders. The only relief was that I wouldn't have to do it much longer.

I bought a bunch of nachos for everyone else, and a bag of Twizzlers for me (the candy that's somehow both boring and good at the same time), and brought it all back to the bleachers. I handed out the nachos, but Jack seemed to zero in on my Twizzlers. So I pulled the bag open and sat next to him, holding the bag out for him to grab one, really wanting to ask him why he was gone today.

"Is this a bribe so I slip your name to my mom in order to get you further up the Founders Scholarship list?" he said, sort of joking, sort of not.

I felt defensiveness bubble into my throat, but instead I shoved the bag closer to him. "It's because I want to give you a Twizzler."

He stared at the bag for a minute, then finally reached inside and pulled one out. "Twizzlers are weird. They're bland, but I can't stop eating them."

I laughed. "I was just thinking that! How do they do that?"

Ashton reached over, shoving his whole hand into the Twizzlers bag, talking to LiQui in depth about every season of *The Real Housewives of New Jersey*. He pulled out a firewood-size clump of Twizzlers without even a look. I squeezed my near-empty bag, feeling its crinkly emptiness. I was suddenly overcome by a dose of sad. "My Twizzlers," I said, not really to anyone.

And Jack started laughing. Hard. "That was the most tragic thing I've seen in forever. Your face. Oh. Ash!"

Ashton whipped around, two Twizzlers sticking out of his mouth. "What?"

"You just took half of Clara's Twizzlers and she's over here ready to break."

Everyone turned to look at me, and suddenly my Twizzler sadness was making everyone laugh, and then I was laughing, and before I knew it Ashton was making his way back from the SnackBox with three bags of Twizzlers, dropping them all in my lap.

Between Jack and me, we ate them all.

## MOJO PLUS TWO

I was shocked at how normal it felt to have two star-stars eating queso with us. LiQui sat next to Jack, Ashton next to me. And, halfway through, Resi came and sat with us. Despite Ashton's earlier reports of everyone being mad at everyone, they didn't seem to be. It was an integration that should've been awkward, but it wasn't. They were humans. They were like me and LiQui, their own crew, and I couldn't stop thinking about that.

I'd thought that LiQui and I were such a singularity, that no one else in the school could've ever matched how tight we were, but watching Ashton, Jack, and Resi interact was like turning a light on.

These two weren't star-stars because they wanted to be

exclusive jackholes. They were the star-stars like LiQui and I were me and LiQui. It was just how it was. I couldn't say this about all the star-stars, but these three? Their exclusivity was a front at worst, or imagined by everyone else at best, and all it took to learn that was looking instead of assuming.

## THE DEATH OF A BATTERY: A MEMOIR

The Monday after Mojo with the star-stars, the news hadn't broken, Mr. Caywell wasn't back, and the library closing had set in at LA. Students weren't just whispering; they were feeling its lack. They were making it a problem for Mr. Walsh, which I felt pretty good about. I especially felt its absence. I didn't know what it was about the library's closing, but simply that it was gone made everyone want books. Books I didn't even have. Books that weren't even banned. Classic greener-grass syndrome.

We always wanted what we couldn't have.

The week before felt like a vacation compared to the amount of Unlib work I was doing now that the library was closed and it made the week go ridiculously fast. So fast

I couldn't keep up. I didn't eat lunch. I was nearly late to every class. If I wasn't sneaking people books in the halls, I was meeting them at my locker. By a water fountain. In the bathroom. Behind a locker door. That week, I did so much app tapping that the fresh, 100-percent-charged battery I'd start the day with went sub–30 percent by lunchtime.

I'd mastered the quick exchange of book and information. I felt well-oiled, but it was so exhausting. I didn't see LiQui at all. And every day, I'd planned on using my free period to write some sort of bad draft speech for the Founders Scholarship Dinner that was barreling toward me. But I didn't. Instead, I scrambled to finish homework mere minutes before it was due. On Wednesday, the ink on a five-page paper about the origins of the black-pepper trade for history class was still warm and smudgeable as I turned it in.

By the time I walked out of school on Thursday, LiQui's and Ashton's lockers were empty, and there were only four books left in mine. Four. *Cuatro.* The same amount of letters in most cuss words was how many books I had left. I'd loaned out sixty-six books. Despite the confusion

I'd had about running the Unlib, I was happy that, in its last days, it was maxed out. People were reading. And it was good. I was everyone's book girl. There was maybe one degree of separation between Lupton Academy's weed guy and me. I considered reaching out for a partnership.

No, I didn't.

That was a joke. I didn't do that.

What I did do after that Thursday was go home, talk to my parents about the Founders Scholarship Dinner, which caused a minor freak-out between the two of them, understandably, considering it was the first they'd heard of it and the event was a paltry two days away. I grabbed a granola bar from the pantry and then excused myself from dinner in order to write my speech, or, if nothing else, stare at a wall and consider the universe. Maybe deal with the self-loathing that would come up when I couldn't think of anything to write about. Luckily, I didn't have to deal with any self-loathing, because I was so exhausted from the day I fell asleep on the desk in my room.

## THE CATCHER WASN'T THERE

*I felt so lonesome, all of a sudden. I almost wished I was dead.*

—J. D. Salinger, *The Catcher in the Rye*

My phone buzzed against the desk. My eyes snapped open. It took a few seconds for me to come around to the fact that it was dark, and that I'd drooled all over the piece of paper that was supposed to be my speech, which felt right.

I rubbed my eyes. My phone started buzzing again. I picked it up.

"Hello?"

A panicked Ashton was on the other end, his breath heavy, filled with fear.

"Ashton?" I said, feeling my brain light on fire and

adrenaline trickle into my chest. "Ashton?"

"I'm just standing here," he said through the tears. "I called 911, but they're not here yet. I'm just standing here and he's lying on the floor."

I stood. "What? What is going on?"

"Jack, I think he's, like . . . I don't know. He's not breathing. There are pill containers everywhere. I think he's dead."

I felt heavier. My head felt twice its size.

"You called 911? Where are you?"

"I'm at school."

"What?" I asked.

"He broke into school and sent me a text about ending it. Something about having no catcher in the rye."

My heart sank. Deep. Deepest. "Ashton. I'll be right there."

"No. Don't come."

"I'll be there soon. Stay on the phone with me."

I ran down the stairs, grabbing the keys from the hook by the door and jumping into my car. If I hadn't handed Jack *Catcher in the Rye*, and we'd simply had the Twizzlers the week before, would we have still ended up here?

The phone was just the sound of Ashton breathing, and maybe a minute after I got in my car, the sounds of paramedics. Ashton talking to them. I drove and listened. The whole world felt cavernous. I was engulfed in pulsing terror. I remembered the night we'd had last week. Eating Twizzlers at the football game. Laughing. But I also remembered our conversation in the processing room.

I'd done this.

I sped to school, arriving to a scene of swirling lights, the darkness a flashing mash of red and blue. Principal Walsh and Jack's mom and dad stood on the stairs. Ashton sat on a small patch of grass off to the side of the paver path. Watching from the shadows as the paramedics wheeled Jack out of the door, down the path, through the roundabout, and into the ambulance.

"Ashton?" I said softly.

He looked up. "Hey."

I sat down next to him.

"He spray-painted something above the library wall, where I found him," he said. "'To Holden Caulfield, from Holden Caulfield. This is my statement.'

"What does it mean?" he asked.

"I don't know," I lied, as guilt oozed out from every pore.

It felt like a knife in the gut, twisting and cutting all the way to the dustiest corners of me. It was the statement written by Mark David Chapman, the shooter of the Beatles' John Lennon, in a copy of *Catcher in the Rye* he had in his pocket when he was arrested for murder. But for Jack? It meant something else. It meant that this was his solution. Holden's was to check into a mental hospital. Jack's was to end it all. This wasn't like in Queso, where people simply disagreed about a book; this was bad. This was damage.

"This was my fault," I said. "I gave him that book. I thought it would help. I didn't think it could do this. I didn't know."

I started crying. Ashton pulled me into him and held me there. He started crying too. Neither of us knew what to say. I was unsure how a book could convince separate someones of both murder and suicide. The thought, the situation, was so jarring that when I glanced at Mr. Walsh, I wondered if he'd been right all along and I'd finally seen what he saw when he looked at books. Unpredictable power.

And I was afraid.

For the first time in my life.

I was afraid of books.

## WHITE COVER UNCOVERED

*A new sickness invaded Jerry, the sickness of knowing what he had become, another animal, another beast, another violent person in a violent world, inflicting damage, not disturbing the universe but damaging it.*

—Robert Cormier, *The Chocolate War*

It was Friday morning. The last day of the Unlib. I hadn't gone back to sleep when I got home. I should've used the time to write a speech for the Founders Scholarship Dinner, but every time I tried to think of something, drawing on the experience of my short life, I saw Jack on a stretcher. Every consideration of LitHouse, every attempt at writing about the Tiny Little Libraries, made me feel surrounded by creatures made of shadow and teeth.

Books were all I had. I mean, I had LiQui and my parents, but outside of them? I was made up of books. Now nothing about my life felt right. It had been swallowed in a sea of questions without answers and I felt selfish for thinking it unfair, but I did. When I needed it most, my foundation was missing. I felt like I was floating in outer space. No bearing. No tether. Just there, and those weren't the sort of feelings that won you scholarships.

I was getting into my car to go to school when my phone rang. It was Ashton.

"Hello?" I said.

"Hey."

"Hey."

"So, Jack is okay. He's at the hospital and will need to go to a juvenile rehab center for a few days to be supervised."

"Okay. When can we see him?"

"I don't know," he said. "I'm trying to figure that out."

"He told me. Last week. He told me."

"He came out to you?"

"Yeah."

He took a giant breath of relief. "Clara, I've been sitting with this since the beginning of high school. In the last three years he's been miserable. Downright miserable. And he's so afraid and feels so alone. I pushed him to come out. To come out to his family. And he did. It went horribly. And he's been hurting ever since. I didn't think he'd ever tell anyone ever again."

"He told me Resi knew."

"Yeah, but Resi thinks Jack should do what he feels comfortable doing and doesn't want to push him. That's why we were all in that big fight last week. I was pushing Jack to come out in general because he's destroying himself trying to make it go away. Resi got mad at me for pushing Jack. I yelled at Resi for watching a friend disintegrate and not doing anything about it. She got mad at me for pushing. Jack got mad at the two of us for fighting about him. Anyway. Before this school year started, he told me he wanted to go to your book club. I didn't know why, but I had a guess. I think he had this idea that everyone there was obviously reading stories with gay kids and that you weren't bashing them. So he wanted to go a few times to see how you responded to those stories. I think, if he felt safe enough, he was going to come out there. With people he knew wouldn't be like his family."

I shook my head. "And I yelled at him before the first night was over."

"Yeah, that wasn't great, but in your defense he was mocking you guys. I think he felt like he'd dragged me along and needed to entertain me or something."

"Did I do this, Ashton?"

"I don't know. I mean, maybe, but a lot of people did this. Not just you."

"What can we do for him?"

"I think . . . I don't know. Be there. Accept him? I don't know what else to do. Being around and acceptance is all I've got."

"Okay. I'll see you soon."

"Yeah. See ya."

I hung up, and I kept telling myself it wasn't my fault, but, God, the correlation was too strong. It had started with my hands. I picked out the book. I had Ashton give him the book.

The school had already been cleaned. No sign of the event that had taken place the night before. I walked into Honors Lit feeling stunned. Sluggish. So lost in the expanse that I wondered why I'd even come. I sat next to Ashton. I knew he felt the same. I reached over and grabbed his hand. I knew LiQui would've freaked out, thinking I was about to start making out with him, but it wasn't like that—despite the number of books I've read where, right then, if my life had been a book, Ashton and I would've gotten together. Then, instantly, everything would have gotten fixed. Pigs would have flown. And all the readers would be rooting for a kiss a few pages later. This wasn't like that.

It was just . . . gender sort of took a back seat, replaced simply by the fact that he was my friend and I wanted to be there for him and that was the best way I knew how.

Class had barely started when someone knocked on the classroom door, then pushed it open. It was Ms. Borgen, the school administrator.

Ms. Skirty SkirtSkirt turned toward the door. "Yes, Mrs. Borgen?"

"Principal Walsh would like to see Ashton Bricks."

My head snapped to Ashton.

He looked right at me, and then at his bag.

My heart sank. I'd checked out *A House of Wooden Windows* and *Speak*—again—to him yesterday after school. *Speak* because he wanted to grab some quotes from it. *House* because he wanted to read Lukas's other book. It wasn't lost on me that the Unlib was going to fall because of the book that had made me want to work in a library in the first place, and that burned fierce.

"Can't it wait, Mrs. Borgen? We're in the middle of class."

"Principal Walsh said it was urgent."

I wanted to bolt toward an exit. Jump out a window. Faint, maybe.

Ashton grabbed his backpack and gave me another look. This one said, *I'm so sorry.*

I returned one that, I hoped, didn't say what I felt.

After he left, panic, not the fog of the night before, kept me from paying attention to class. Was Mr. Walsh reaming Ashton out for being a burr in the blanket of school pride? Was Ashton spilling all the secrets of the Unlib? I knew he wouldn't, but maybe it didn't matter if he did. If Mr. Walsh knew about the white covers, the operation was no longer covert. Incognito was out the door.

For the first time since I'd started it, I realized how stupid I'd been. Not because of my romantic hope of winning Mr. Walsh over with quotes, or even of—quotes aside—just winning the battle of books against him, but because I'd put my Founders Scholarship chances at risk the moment I started. I hadn't thought I'd end up here. It was all supposed to be a silent war. Running in the background. None of it was what I'd thought would happen, but, at the same time, I hadn't known what I thought would happen. Why had I done this to myself?

Then, in the middle of Honors Lit, the same place I'd been inspired to start the Unlib, I realized something.

Books had always been such a positive part of my life, an only-ever-good thing I was praised for being into. So when someone else said, "No, these aren't good for you," I got angry. Now that anger had been replaced by worry and confusion, I wondered for the first time what reason someone could've had to say they weren't good for me.

I'd felt off about the Unlib from the day it started because I'd never questioned books before. I'd always thought that if it was book-shaped, it was good. My mom and dad had affirmed as much. In the same way, I'd never questioned what books actually did to me. For me. With me. My whole life, I'd only seen the world open its arms to books. But suddenly I had Mr. Walsh saying that they weren't good for me to read? I'd had no idea someone could look at a book and think it would make them, or anyone else that read it, worse off. I'd had no idea someone wouldn't want someone else to read something.

And it had bothered me.

Why?

Why?

What was I missing?

And now I finally saw it.

Damage.

I wasn't Levi.

I wasn't Joss.

I wasn't Katniss.

I wasn't Guy Montag.

I wasn't Lila.

I'd thought I was when all of this started. Instead . . .

I was naive.

I was wrong.

## THE EVERYWHERE OF FRIENDS

*Oh, Celie, unbelief is a terrible thing. And so is the hurt we cause others unknowingly.*

—Alice Walker, *The Color Purple*

I was walking toward my next class after Honors Lit when the PA sparked to life. Every single student stopped, eyes fixed on the ceiling as if we could find some sort of hint of what was about to be said in the metal mesh covering the speakers.

"Attention, staff and students." It was Mr. Walsh. "There will be an emergency assembly held in the gym in ten minutes. I repeat, there will be an emergency assembly in the gym in ten minutes. All staff and students should make their way there as soon as possible. Attendance is mandatory. Again, there will be an emergency rally in the gym in ten minutes. Attendance is mandatory. Thank you."

It seemed too coincidental to not have anything to do with the Unlib. Ashton hadn't come back to class. A small part of me hoped the assembly would be about Jack. Maybe Mr. Walsh would ream everyone out for having pushed Jack into the dirt every day for three years, like I had.

"Hey," Ashton said, behind me.

I turned around. Before he could say anything, I hugged him and broke down at the same time.

"What happened?" I finally got out.

"Too much to explain," he said, and before I could ask anything else, LiQui was there with her StuCab, moving me out of the middle of the hall, where every Tom, Dick, and student was walking by a sobbing, wrong Clara.

"I'm over," I said finally. "It's done." I told everyone about how panicked I was when Ashton got pulled from class. I told them about my plan to quit the Unlib. And I wished so, so much I'd quit sooner. At my first hesitation.

I didn't finish my thoughts; I was interrupted by the screeching PA reminding me that there was an emergency assembly in the gym and that attendance was, I repeat, mandatory.

"Guys, just . . . promise me that you'll still hang out with me when I go to a new school? When you go to college?" I asked, wiping the tears from my eyes. "Promise me I won't lose you."

Everything pushed against my nerves. It felt like, if even the slightest of breezes came, I'd tip.

LiQui wrapped her arms around me. "Trouble goes everywhere," LiQui said, "but so do I."

Ashton nodded. "We."

"We're here," LiQui said, hand on my shoulder. "Sometimes we'll be there, anywhere, or everywhere, but even then we'll be here."

I nodded.

"You got this, Clara," Scott said. "You're the most badass book chick I know."

I wiped a tear. "You don't know any other book chicks. Besides, I don't know if I want to be a book chick anymore."

"That's fine," LiQui said. "Let the Mav take over."

We all laughed, me again while wiping my eyes. And then, holding LiQui's hand, with Ashton's arm wrapped around my shoulders, I walked toward my future.

## THAT'S MY QUOTE

*I found bravery here.*

—Resi Alistair, *on white cover BB*

Mr. Walsh stood in the center of the half-court circle, hands held behind his back. There was not a single fidget or twitch to be found. All his frustrating quirky congeniality had been drained desert dry. He looked like I'd always thought he should look. Mad. Aggressive. It was the true Mr. Walsh. Not the fake one we'd always seen wandering the halls.

He held a white cover under his arm.

The bleachers had been pulled from the walls, offering their hard edges as seats. Because of my crying fest, we were some of the last kids to walk in, and because we were some of the last, we had to sit in the second row. Practically eye level with Mr. Walsh.

A crew flanked me. Ashton on one side, LiQui and the StuCab on the other. Then, as the last of the students filed in, Resi came over from her spot and sat behind me. Then the Mav. Taking the first row. Sitting in front of me. His mass blocking me, mostly, from the eyes of Mr. Walsh. I looked around, surrounded by people I'd never thought would surround me. Confused as to why anyone but LiQui was there.

The last student took her seat, and Principal Walsh started to speak.

"As you know, a certain discipline must be maintained in a school." He paused for a second, as if he was taken aback by his own words. "It has come to my attention that there is a group of books circulating the school that look like this." He held up the book for all to see. I wasn't sure who in the crowd would or wouldn't recognize it. I'd given out so many over the past weeks it was hard to know who'd been a patron and who hadn't.

"If you're not aware," he said, "these books are on the

list of prohibited media, which is stated in the student handbook."

No one said anything about the fact that there *wasn't* a list in the student handbook. LiQui was right. Either no one read it—most likely—or no one noticed.

Principal Walsh continued. "Having prohibited media is unacceptable and will be punished. We must know the importance of adhering to this rule, so I'm increasing the punishment until we can all remember that it isn't funny, nor is it prudent, or best for the well-being of the student body, to break the rules, especially with prohibited media." He held it up. "I've already suspended one student, and I am prepared to suspend more."

Ashton.

He'd been suspended because of me. I'd tipped Jack over the edge. The amount of damage I'd done, that books had done, was already too costly. I turned to Ashton. He hadn't told me. He caught my eye and waved me off. How could he be so blasé?

"After the end of classes, on your way out of school, we will be checking your person for any prohibited media, and anyone caught with one of these books will be immediately suspended. However, I will give you a simple warning if you turn them in between the end of this assembly and the end of the school day. It's your choice. Another thing. There is a quote written on this book: 'I found bravery here.' I'd like to say to the person who wrote this: You are in danger of falling down a slippery slope. There are reasons these books are prohibited. You should reconsider your judgments and ask yourself if you've really considered what is appropriate for consumption.

"Now, I'd like to offer one more thing. If the person, or persons, responsible for these books steps forward, they will save their classmates the trouble of suspension, and I'll reverse any suspensions I've hitherto dealt. To that person I say: It is your choice. If you truly care about your community and their well-being, you'll take responsibility for your actions."

Some girl raised her hand. "Isn't banning books wrong?"

"Prohibiting media is well within the reaches of private-school policy. Your administration has decided what is most conducive to your formation and growth as a student, and your job is to trust and honor the policies we've set into place."

I wanted to cry right there. I wanted to run away. I had to turn myself in. Ashton had been suspended. It didn't matter to me if anyone else got suspended. Ashton didn't deserve it. Not in his senior year. After being a friend to Jack.

"Any other questions?" he asked, glancing over the student body. "Then that is all," Mr. Walsh said. "I trust many of you will do the right thing. Now, please go to your classes and sit and wait. Faculty and staff, please stay here for a few moments. We'll need to discuss logistics for the end of the day."

Would I miss enough school that I'd have to repeat my senior year? Would I have to watch LiQui graduate and go to college without me? Would I lose the Founders Scholarship? Would I even go to college?

It didn't matter. I needed to turn myself in. I was wrong. I knew that. I was wrong.

I stood, ready to walk down to him, when the Mav pushed me back, then stood. "Principal Walsh, that's my quote on the book. Not only that, I started this."

Principal Walsh looked at him, confused, not willing to write him off, but also in disbelief. No. This isn't how it'd go. The Mav wasn't going to take the fall for my stupidity.

"No," I said. "It wasn't him. I wrote that quote. I started this. I've bee—"

Before I finished, Ashton stood. "That's my quote. I started this."

I looked at him, almost feeling betrayed. Why would he do that? He was already in trouble. In fact, he didn't even need to be at this assembly. He was suspended. He didn't need to be in more trouble. Why would he be so stupid as to throw himself into a fray he had no place in? This was my problem.

I opened my mouth to stop it, but then LiQui stood, interrupting me. "That's my quote. I did this. I started it."

Resi stood.

The StuCab stood.

Then someone on the opposite side of the bleachers stood. Someone I didn't know. "That's my quote."

Suddenly, student after student stood, faces I somewhat recognized, some I didn't, all saying that it was their quote, a statement that seemed to take on the meaning *It was me.*

It wasn't like one of those movies where the whole room

stood, but it felt like it. In truth, it was a smattering of students. Probably forty or so out of our class of five hundred. All my friends, a bunch of patrons I recognized but didn't know, and all twelve of my classmates from Honors Lit.

In contrast, those who stood seemed swallowed by those who didn't, but with each new student taking credit for the Unlib, Principal Walsh got more and more frustrated, his path forward growing muddier and muddier with red tape and time.

What I didn't understand was, what were those who weren't my friends standing for?

Finally no one else stood up, and the gym was silent for an awkward half minute. One of the star-stars I didn't know raised his hand. "So . . . does that mean the rest of us are free to go?"

The gym echoed in laughter, breaking the intensity of the moment.

But the star-star was right.

The ones who'd stood had turned ourselves in.

Sighing, Mr. Walsh pointed at everyone who stood up. "Those of you who stood must speak to my assistant and set up a meeting with me before you leave today." As the gym started to break into a clatter of talking and squeaking feet, he stormed out of the gym, his walking frantic.

I looked at everyone who'd stood.

Then I cried.

Mad. Confused. Happy.

Not alone.

## AND YOUR HERO GOES HOME EARLY

*We loaded books into a mine cart. Tossing them without care. Armies and their weapons in front of our cave. There was no time for care. "Levi, go ahead and push this one ahead," I said. He strained against the cart. It moved slowly. A screechy metallic whine echoing through the cave. He flashed me a smile. One that said, we're doing this, but then a black Westland coat appeared on the tracks, and Levi was looking at me, smiling, when a bullet lodged in his heart.*

—Lukas Gebhardt, *Don't Tread on Me*

Right after the assembly, instead of going to class, I went straight to Mr. Walsh's assistant to set up the meeting, and then I left. I was completely drained of any ability to stand on my own two feet. I didn't want to see the line of kids dropping off the white covers at the end of the day, turning them in, wondering on each handover if my name was going to come up. I didn't want to see the blockade at the front of the door. I didn't want to see all the people who'd stood up for me.

So I ran. I left the Unlib to be torn apart.

So unlike Levi and Joss.

I ran up to my room, the house silent, Mom and Dad both at work, not knowing that their daughter had wasted their time and money by getting expelled her senior year and throwing away her shot at an amazing scholarship in the process. I lay on my bed. What did it mean that a group of us had turned ourselves in? Would I even be able to take credit for the Unlib? Should I? Would Ashton still be suspended? Maybe it didn't matter that everyone had stood. Principal Walsh would figure it out. It was a matter of time. People borrowed books from me, no one else. Someone would spill that eventually.

## THE FIRST GROUP TEXT

**Ashton** [8:22 PM] C, did you leave?

I found out Jack has some visiting hours open tomorrow.

Would you be up for going with me?

Also, is it okay that I'm texting LiQui?

**Me** [8:22 PM] I can't go. It's the Founders Scholarship Dinner

Can we do the next day?

Also, yes I left, I took a nap

**LiQui** [8:23 PM] Yeah, Ashton. I'll go. I'm good with whenever

Also, Clara, probably a good call, TBH

Need to Mojo?

**Me** [8:23 PM] idk

**Ashton** [8:23 PM] Yes. I need Mojo even if Clara doesn't. Sunday has the same visiting hours, so let's do that.

Hey, LiQui . . . did I or did I not see you making out with the Mav by the water fountains after the assembly?

**Me** [8:23 PM] What

**LiQui** [8:23 PM] Ashton, WTF

**Ashton** [8:24 PM] Oh, whoops. Sorry. I thought . . . like . . . I don't know what I thought. Bad way to start our first group text.

**Me** [8:24 PM] What.

**LiQui** [8:24 PM] YOU DON'T JUST SAY THAT SORT OF SHIT ON A GROUP MESSAGE

**Me** [8:24 PM] It was the Mav standing up for me in the assembly. Wasn't it?

**LiQui** [8:24 PM] Literally the hottest thing he's ever done and he has a six pack and plays football.

**Ashton** [8:24 PM] Mojo in 30?

**LiQui** [8:24 PM] You're paying. Make up for that junk you just pulled.

**Ashton** [8:24 PM] Okay, that's fair.

**Me** [8:24 PM] Okay.

## MOJOVATION (PART TWO)

*But it's the truth even if it didn't happen.*

—Ken Kesey, *One Flew Over the Cuckoo's Nest*

On the table was a purple Mojo plate with a massive bowl of queso.

Despite everything, I couldn't help but smile.

I grabbed a chip, doused it, then laid it on my tongue. Trying to let the melty cheesiness melt away my problems. I turned to LiQui. "So you're back together with the Mav?"

"Hey," she said, putting a hand up. "If you're feeling sass, let it pass."

"No sass. Are you?"

LiQui frowned, obviously still feeling a little defensive.

"Yes—I mean, no. Not really, but look, we're not here to talk about the Mav, so chill."

"Chill?" I snapped. "Chill? I was up at two a.m. last night because I gave a book to Jack that made him decide to kill himself. I got Ashton suspended, and despite everyone's heroics, I'm practically waiting to be expelled. When I am, I lose my scholarship, I lose everything, and you want me to chill? God, why didn't you make me stop? Why did you let me go through with it? It wasn't worth it."

No one said anything for a while; then LiQui said, "That's not fair, and pretty self-righteous, Clara."

"What do you mean, that's not fair? You're not—"

"The Unlib was just as much ours as it was yours," she said. "We supported you. Fought with you, *for* you, so much that the 'you' turned into 'us.' All that research I did in contract law, trying to find loopholes that would let us fight the banned list? All the brainstorming? That was my choice. Not only that, but you got me planning on standing up to my grandparents. You got the Mav wanting to get back together because he read *Eleanor and Park*. You've got Ashton here. Like right here. A friend who you've obviously helped, otherwise he wouldn't be here. Scott told me the other day he hasn't stopped reading since I gave him *Perks*. The dominoes, girl. Have you looked at the dominoes? And who knows what other things have happened that we don't even know about?"

"I know Resi's changed because of it," Ashton added. "And Jack was happy that night. The night at the football game. I know he was. I hadn't seen him laugh in a long time."

LiQui continued. "You can't know what else has happened because of the Unlib. So before you go telling us that it wasn't worth it, why don't you actually look around? Sure, some things haven't turned out great, but we've all made the choices we've made because *we* made them. You didn't force Ashton to check out a book and therefore get caught. To think you're responsible for all the damage is pretty insulting to the rest of us. Especially Jack. You're literally chalking what he did up to you, completely ignoring whatever else he was going through."

LiQui looked at me with a face that told me to step up and challenge her. She was ready for a fight. But it wasn't that what she said didn't make sense to me; it just seemed inconsequential. Jack had tried to kill himself because of

what he got from a book. Was that not terrifying to anyone else? Did no one else see how not in control we were of
books and what they did to people?

Ashton raised his hand. "Can I add something?"

LiQui waved a hand at me. I nodded.

"I'm not, like, a book guy, but isn't the point of all this
book stuff like what Ms. Croft was teaching us—that
unrestricted access to books allows us to be challenged
and changed? To learn new things and to critically think
about those things and not be afraid of them? To be better
than we were before we read them?"

I shrugged. I didn't know. I wasn't sure anymore, and
that settled around me like a crash-landing spaceship and
the dust of a villain's retreat. We could talk about romantic ideas of books all we wanted, but that didn't explain
the friend in the hospital. Nothing did. Jack hadn't been
thinking critically. He hadn't had the space to think critically. So . . . like, maybe calling a book "inappropriate" for
someone to read was a right thing.

I didn't know.

And not knowing shook me down to my bone marrow.

# A NOT-FANCY EMAIL FOR CLARA

Part A: The Email

To: clara.evans@luptonacademy.edu

From: m.walsh@luptonacademy.edu

Subject: IMPORTANT: Monday Morning

Ms. Evans,

Just a reminder that I'll see you at my office first thing Monday morning. This time, I'll leave it to you to speak to your parents about this matter.

Principal Walsh

Part B: My Subsequent Reaction

To: m.walsh@luptonacademy.edu

From: clara.evans@luptonacademy.edu

Subject: RE: IMPORTANT: Monday Morning


OK.

## THE DREARY-WEARIES

*There are things you can't back down on, things you gotta take a stand on. But it's up to you to decide what them things are.*

—Mildred D. Taylor, *Roll of Thunder, Hear My Cry*

I couldn't sleep.

I couldn't stop thinking about Jack, and it kept me distracted from the fact that I still didn't have a speech for the Founders Scholarship Dinner, and that, really, it didn't matter if I had one or not.

On Monday, I was as good as expelled.

## SURPRISES OVER MAGNOLIAS

*He called her beautiful, but he'd also called the book in her hands inappropriate. Lila thought the last was a negation of the first. For when one called a book too ugly for the world, one negated all the beauty found within. Books could have ugly parts, but no book was ugly through and through. If he couldn't see that about her book, then she deduced he'd never be able to see that about her.*

—Lukas Gebhardt, *A House of Wooden Windows*

I wore a knee-length black dress with a V neckline that showed off a pearl necklace I'd borrowed from my mom. I also had matching earrings and a simple pair of black ankle-strap heels. My stomach was roiling, and I felt constantly on the verge of throwing up. My parents and

I walked into the Hunter Museum of Art, a building of sculpture made of metal and glass. It stood above the Tennessee River like a watchman. Its walls teased the edge of an eighty-foot bluff that disappeared into the curves of the river.

I was silent as we walked through the entrance, a wall of windows. A long line of black stanchions led us past the exhibition wings and into a grand foyer. It felt super fancy. Flagstone floors. Eight circular tables were covered in spotless black tablecloths with green runners. In their centers stood great glass cylinders wrapped in burlap ribbon bows and filled with magnolia leaves and cotton buds. A sweeping staircase, metal curvature on one side and glass partition on the other, led to a second floor where you could stand above the foyer, watch the people below, or get a better view from the massive walls of windows overlooking the blue trusses and rivets of the Walnut Street Bridge, the North Shore, the river horizon, and a small island bisecting the ancient currents. I saw a patio that extended off the grand foyer, which, I decided, would be a great place to go if I needed to throw up. It was far enough away from the hubbub, unlit, that no one would notice a girl in pearls hurling her fancy dinner into a river.

It was a Goldilocks evening, with a just-right breeze and a just-right chill that felt almost like a fall night instead of the end of summer. Despite the perfection in weather, I knew the night would be far from perfect.

My parents didn't know anything I was feeling. They were there with a look of pride in their eyes. A look that killed me every time they said a word to me. I remembered our conversation the night I'd gotten the first strike, how adamant my mom had been about not bending the rules. How adamant I'd been about being the one who made the choices, and there I was, at a dinner, with no speech because I'd already lost.

I couldn't tell them.

I couldn't tell them any of it. If I wasn't going to have the night, then I wanted them to. It was the least I could do before they found out their daughter was expelled from school.

"This is incredible," Dad said, looking around. "It feels like you're the president already."

"Whoa," I said, feigning happy. "I'm not the president. LiQui is."

"No one said you both couldn't be the president. You just have to choose who goes first."

"You two are going to get us kicked out," Mom said. "Act fancier."

"This is all I got," I said, waving a hand down myself.

Dad nodded in agreement and said, "What she said."

We found an empty table with a small paper card, emblazoned with the number six, sticking out of the magnolia leaves. After confirming it was ours, we sat down, no guest of distinction to be seen. I couldn't even remember who mine was.

I looked around the room, curious as to who the other Founders Scholarship finalists were. I'd only ever known that Jack was one, but he wasn't there.

To my surprise, the only other person I recognized was Resi Alistair. She sat at table two with her family. We locked eyes and she waved; then, to my surprise, she stood up and walked toward me. I told my parents I'd be right back.

We stopped in front of each other.

"I didn't know you were a finalist," I said.

"Well, I wasn't. I was a runner-up. They called me after

Jack was disqualified."

"Oh," I said. "Why was he disqualified?"

"I don't know specifics. I'm assuming, despite his family's best attempts at keeping everything quiet, the publicness of his attempt and all the stuff that came before forced the selection committee to take him out? I don't know. I just know Mrs. Lodenhauer is probably on fire with anger."

I sighed. It wasn't fair. He should've been there. "Have you seen him yet?"

"I haven't yet, no. I'm going to go tomorrow."

I nodded. "Oh, well why don't you come with us? We're going tomorrow."

"Yeah. Ashton mentioned that. That sounds good."

We were silent for a second; then she put a hand on my shoulder. "Thank you."

"Thank you?" I asked.

"For everything."

I tried not to look too dumbstruck, but I literally couldn't think of a single thing I'd done that Resi should/ would be thanking me for.

"You've been . . . a miracle this year. I mean, not even

that—even before with what you did with your Tiny Little Libraries."

Because I was raised in a barn, my eyebrows shot up in disbelief and I didn't say thank you.

She laughed. "When you launched LitHouse, you were the talk of my community-leadership group. You inspired me to do the project that got me here."

My jaw dropped. I had no idea what to say.

"But what I really want to say thank you for is the friend you've been to Ashton and Jack. I—I haven't been able to be there for either of them in a lot of what's happened, and it's been so nice to know that you have."

"Resi," I laughed, "I wasn't there for them—Jack just came to me. I mean, thank you, but I'm not as awesome as you think I am. LitHouse is just LitHouse. I'm like wondering if I've been doing the wrong thing. I don't know."

It was her turn to be dumbstruck. "Why would you think LitHouse is a wrong thing?"

"Because I don't trust books anymore. They obviously hurt people."

She frowned. "Is this because of the Unlib? Are you

letting the stuff at Lupton affect you that much?"

"It's not just Lupton, Resi—it's my life. All I've ever done is books, and with Jack . . . I don't know anymore."

"Clara, you have nothing to do with Jack. I mean, maybe a little bit, but he can take anything and make it negative. It's where he's been at for a while. Not that he doesn't have his reasons. Anyway, the night after the first football game of the year, when Jack got that DUI? It splintered our friend group." She paused. Took a breath. "Ashton and I almost gave up on him with the rest of the group, but we didn't. Do you want to know why? *Speak.* I know *Speak* was about a different topic, but it was also about someone who hurt so bad it shaded every second of their life. It was the exact story we needed to keep going. What if your library hadn't been there? What if we hadn't had that book right then, right when we needed it? We would've given up. Maybe Jack wouldn't have had anyone to text Thursday night. Principal Walsh can ban books as much as he wants, with whatever justification he wants, but the books in your library altered space and time. There's undeniable proof the books you handed out impacted the world around you."

She looked at me, her eyes pleading with mine to hear her.

"But I started the Unlib all wrong, too," I added. "It wasn't because I was, like, this book warrior who wanted peers to have access to books—like I was when I started LitHouse. I started the Unlib because I was mad. I wanted to be right. I wanted to win. Books were my weapons."

"I mean, yeah, that's not great, but it doesn't matter. I don't mean this the way it sounds, but you're not that important. You weren't the one responsible for the change. The books were. They didn't need you to be angelic and perfect. They needed you to be willing to pass them along. You've been helping this happen for years, not just with your Unlib. Think about your Tiny Little Libraries. If this small library in your locker has done so much in such a short amount of time, think about what those have done. Books are wild things. You can't tame them. People are wild things. You can't tame them, either. Put those two together and you can't know what's going to happen, but that's not on you. And if you're going to get into the 'if it's appropriate for students' debate, leave it up to the parents. That's why they exist. There. Done. Move on. Wipe your hands of it."

I stared at her. Not sure what to say. I could probably have said thank you, but it wasn't anywhere near my
tongue and I didn't know where to find it.

"Sorry," she said. "I just . . . I don't want you to give up. I
want you to know you've done a lot. Even if you don't think
you have. Thank you."

I stared at my feet. I didn't feel like that person.

"Who's the guest at your table tonight?" she asked.

I couldn't remember, so I shrugged. "I can't remember.
It's been a crazy few wee—"

"I am," someone said. An older woman, walking up to
me from the side.

She stared at Resi with coldness even I could feel.

Resi faked a smile. "Mrs. Lodenhauer, nice to see you."

Right.

Mrs. Lodenhauer.

Mrs. Janet Lodenhauer.

My mind flashed back to the email I'd gotten last week.
I hadn't even noticed.

Jack's mom was my guest of distinction, and simply by
how she stood, by the way she looked at me, I knew she
wasn't happy about it. And there was only one reason for

her not to be happy with me. She knew that I was the dealer of *Catcher in the Rye*.

She blamed me for Jack.

My stomach sank for the millionth time.

Mrs. Lodenhauer didn't respond to Resi. Everything she did emanated cold disdain for her, as if she blamed Resi as well.

Mrs. Lodenhauer looked at me. "I'd like to speak with you."

Resi reached for my arm. Placing her hand on my wrist in a gesture that I could only understand as *I'm sorry*. She smiled. "Come find me after." She gave a curt wave to Mrs. Lodenhauer. "Nice seeing you, Mrs. Lodenhauer."

Then she walked away, leaving me with the coldest potion of anger, bitterness, and dissatisfaction I'd ever met.

## TORN TO THREADS

*When people don't express themselves, they die one piece at a time. You'd*
*be shocked at how many adults are really dead inside—walking through*
*their days with no idea who they are, just waiting for a heart attack or*
*cancer or a Mack truck to come along and finish the job. It's the saddest*
*thing I know.*

—Laurie Halse Anderson, *Speak*

Mrs. Lodenhauer walked away from me without saying
a word, but she did so with the expectation that I'd follow, which made me not want to follow. In fact, everything
about her made me not want to follow and also made me
feel even worse for Jack. Knowing how rotten she was.
You didn't even need to talk to her to figure that out. And,

yeah, her son had just tried to take his life, that wasn't a thing to be happy about, but there was so much of her anger that was timeless, a foul smell of a long rottenness in the snap of her step as she walked up the stairs to the top floor.

On my way, my parents waved to me as if I was winning the lottery. I waved back, but I can't remember what my face looked like. Was it happy? Probably not. I don't think I even tried to smile.

Upstairs. She led me to the point farthest away from everyone, then spun around and glowered at me for a few seconds. "Who do you think you are?"

The snap was so surprising that the only thing that came out was, "Who do *you* think I am?"

Her lip curled. "You don't think I know about your book? That garbage I found in his room wrapped in white paper?"

I said nothing.

"Jack told me you gave it to him. You can't play dumb with me, Clara. I know about everything, and anything I know, Principal Walsh knows. So it's time for you to be honest. The library. You dealing books out of your locker.

Let me ask you again. Who do you think you are?"

I shrugged, hearing my fate on Monday lock into place. "I honestly don't know, ma'am."

"You're a rule breaker," she said. "Someone who thinks it's okay and even worth fighting for the right to shove trash into other kids' hands. My husband's grandfather would've died of a heart attack if he knew what you've done. The Lodenhauer legacy is Lupton Academy. I went there. My husband went there. We've given millions of dollars. We've built Lupton Academy with our money. It would be nothing without us." She paused, her nostrils flaring. "You know how long I fought with Principal Walsh to expand the banned-book list?"

She took a step closer to me. "He didn't want to deal with the politics, but everyone has a price, and his was SPA. So we made a deal. We gave Lupton money to buy SPA. I bought that banned list. Because of what books do to children. And here you come, thinking you have something to say about how my family has run the school since its inception. And look what you did. Your imprudence, your lack of respect for authority, your lack of sight when it comes to what books are appropriate, has put my son in a mental institution. I should make you pay for the SPA deal. I should make you pay for his college. Because you cost him his shot at the Founders Scholarship. He'd be here if it weren't for you. You are the very reason the banned-book list was put into place. You've lived your life for books, and look at you. You shove your ideas on everyone else. You're a moral disaster. You may have tricked the panel into believing that you deserve this award, but you aren't important. You have nothing to say. Your books have done nothing but hurt people. All your knowledge will be useful when you can only get a job as a fry cook at McDonald's."

I was crying. Somewhere between her first word and the end of the first sentence, I started. But I forced myself to cry silently. To not give her the satisfaction of hearing her swings land hard.

"What you are is useless and unformed, and you and I both know that, come Monday, all of this will be gone. So why are you here? You shouldn't have even come. Save us all the ten minutes of worthless chatter you're planning to give and go. It should've been you in the mental hospital. Not Jack. He was a bystander in your destruction—"

"I'd say that's quite enough," my dad said, appearing

by my side. "Ma'am, I don't know who you are, and at this moment I don't really care. If you say one more word to my daughter, I promise you neither you nor I will like the result."

Mrs. Lodenhauer scoffed, then tugged on her ear. Speaking to the floor, she said, "I see where she gets her demeanor from."

Dad smiled. "Yes, and I'm very proud of her for it. Now, I respectfully ask that you never talk to my daughter again."

"Good luck with what's left of your school year," Mrs. Lodenhauer said as my dad pulled me away. He brought me down to Mom, and he kept asking me what Mrs. Lodenhauer had been talking about, but I was too tied up in my thoughts. So tied up that by the time I sat back down at our table, my tears had dried up. I wouldn't spill tears for that. She was lost. But who wasn't? She had no right. She wasn't right.

While she yelled at me, something shifted in my heart. Suddenly, I knew the choice Jack had made was so much more than the message he got from a book. His heart was wrapped with layers and layers of hurt. I saw a part of where that came from firsthand as his mom tore me to shreds. It felt so unjust to give *Catcher in the Rye* any credit for bringing Jack to the edge when there was someone like Janet Lodenhauer tearing him down daily. To say his suicide attempt was *Catcher*'s fault—heck, even to say it was *my* fault—would let Janet off the hook. There was no separating the impact of her life on his, and maybe it's the same for every decision inspired by a book.

The problem is, we bring ourselves to the pages. Our whole selves. Every single darkness. Every single light. Every single passion. Every single hurt. We read with all the layers that make us who we are acting as filters. We read with all that our eyes have seen and all our hearts have felt since birth. With that much density making up humanity, it can't be up to us to make sure people don't misunderstand a book. And it can't be up to books to make sure people don't kill themselves or hate someone, or even love someone. Or even decide to be president. What we do, before and after we read, is our choice. And that choice is freedom.

I wondered if, maybe, Mrs. Lodenhauer would've been different if she hadn't spent all her life putting out the wrong fires. I couldn't know if there was any correlation between her stance on reading and how rotten and afraid of the world she was. I was sure it wasn't as simple as reducing her problems to the fact that she hadn't read *Catcher in the Rye*, but I did know that it certainly didn't help.

If she had read it, she could've seen that Holden, one of the most loved literary characters of all time, was writing what he'd learned from a mental hospital, and maybe she would've been able to get past the shame she felt for her son and see a new beginning instead.

If she'd read *Don't Tread on Me*, maybe she would've seen Levi and Joss die for something that ultimately united two sides of a war, and maybe she would've seen books as a source of freedom instead of poison.

Maybe, if she'd read *Speak*, she would've simply disagreed with me, not torn me to pieces because she wanted me to suffer.

Maybe, if she'd read *Perks*, she would've seen some of the ways that her son was being mistreated because of his sexual orientation, and been able to suspend her hate for a hot minute to be there for him, to love him, to give him an actual home to come back to.

"Who was that, Clara?" Dad asked again, incredulous. "Why was she speaking to you like that?"

I took a deep breath. "Dad, I'll tell you later. I need to go write my speech."

Both my parents looked at me. Eyes wide as plates. "You haven't written your speech?"

"Clara, the dinner starts in ten minutes," Mom said.

I stood, grabbed a pen from my mom's purse and a handful of cocktail napkins from the hors d'oeuvres table, and rushed to the closest bathroom.

## A QUICK NAPKIN LIST OF THE DOMINOES
## THAT FELL

- Jack Lodenhauer

- Ashton Bricks

- LiQui Carson

- Scott Wieberdink

- Ms. Croft

- Mr. Caywell

- Resi Alistair

- The Mav

- Me

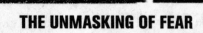

# THE UNMASKING OF FEAR

*Courage is [not] a man with a gun in his hand. It's knowing you're licked before you begin but you begin anyway and you see it through no matter what.*

—Harper Lee, *To Kill a Mockingbird*

I stood at the podium. My eyes were red, but my hands were calm. I looked at Mrs. Lodenhauer, who now sat at a completely different table. I looked at my parents. I looked at Resi. I looked at the faces I didn't know. Journalists. I looked at everyone. My insides were calm.

Most of my moments—good, bad—had happened because I'd let books shape my choices. Even during the last few days, when I was questioning books, they were working, teaching me that they were bigger than my own experience. Teaching me how to see others when I thought I already knew how. Teaching me how to truly believe in them. I was standing in that room because of books, and, thanks to Mrs. Lodenhauer, I was no longer afraid of what they were or weren't.

I'd started the school year in a war. Not a war against Lupton. A war against myself. I'd been selfish. Only thinking about how books impacted me. About how they changed my life. I'd wanted to prove Mr. Walsh wrong because I wanted the proof. Everything I'd done, every choice, had been about me.

I'd gotten so focused on how I fit into the things LA was saying about books that I hadn't even noticed that books were changing everything. LiQui had said as much. I hadn't believed her. But it was true. We'd all been changed. And because books had changed us, they'd also changed the people around us. An impact that could be written off as the simple progression of life. What a power.

Mrs. Lodenhauer, Mr. Walsh, and I weren't that different from one another.

In one way or another, we were afraid. We were afraid

of books, but more than that. We were afraid of ideas, discussions, changes, because we were afraid of what those things could take from us. We were afraid. And I had it on good authority that being afraid was the opposite of being free.

I cleared my throat, fighting the desire to close my eyes. I said, "Hi, I'm Clara Evans. Some of you may know me from the work I've done with the Tiny Little Libraries, but I'm going to talk about that one time my school banned a bunch of books, what happened when I started a banned-book library in my locker, and why it matters."

## A WILD LIBRARIAN APPEARS

I stood outside on a patio overlooking the river, getting some fresh air as the speeches finished inside. I needed a minute alone. To let it all settle. To let everything I'd said in my speech spread roots in my mind and heart.

"Well," someone said, leaning on the railing next to me, "I'm glad I crashed the party, because that was the best speech I've ever heard. I'm so proud of you, Clara."

I turned to see Mr. Caywell. He was all suited up. I guess he knew now what I'd really done with his books.

"Before you ask, I came with my sister. All prior Founders Scholars are invited to the dinner. I knew you'd be speaking, and I wasn't about to miss it."

"Thanks, Mr. Caywell. I owe you an apology."

He raised his eyebrows. "I should be apologizing to you."

I nodded. "Wait . . . why would you apologize to me? I was the one who lied. Remember that first day of school?"

"Yeah?"

"When I said I'd bring the banned books to the Tiny Little Libraries?"

"Yeah?"

"Well . . . I didn't."

"What a surprise," he said flatly.

"Wait . . . why are you being sarcastic?"

"Because at one point, I got one of your white construction paper books in the book-return box. Wasn't hard to figure out what was going on once I pulled the cover off and saw a book *you* were supposed to get rid of."

"Oh." I remembered the day I'd found the book from Hanna Chen in my backpack. I hadn't just forgotten. He'd slipped it into my backpack while I was working on the processing room. "So the whole time you were sending people to me, you knew?"

He shrugged. "And that's why I need to apologize to you. I was going to say something at first, but then I got caught up in all of it. I knew you'd be putting yourself at risk, and I think I ignored that because I felt that, out of all the students, if someone could pull it off without being caught, you could. I should've told you to stop."

"Should you have?"

He turned and looked back out at the river.

"I don't regret it, Mr. Caywell. Not now. Whatever happens happens. Even though it took me a while to figure out, I stood for what was right. For what I believe in. Just like you have done for the last however many years. I've learned so much. Changed. I've got new friends. I've seen them change too. And I don't regret any of it."

He smiled. "See you on Monday?"

I nodded. "After my meeting with Mr. Walsh. It'll probably be my last time volunteering."

"Well, whatever happens," he said, "I'm proud of you, and you deserve to win tonight."

I smiled. Mostly because I felt what I'd said. I actually felt it.

I didn't regret it.

I didn't regret believing that books mattered.

## BROTHER LEON

*Freedom is a tax. We pay it when our ideas are challenged, and we pay it when we challenge the ideas of others.*
*But we must pay.*
*And we must pay gladly, knowing that to have it any other way would be to lose freedom itself.*

—Lukas Gebhardt, *Don't Tread on Me*

It was Monday. Probably my last day at LA.

I stared at his door, remembering that all my friends, even Ashton, were waiting for me at the library. If nothing else, I'd still have them. Schools didn't dictate friendships.

I knocked on his door.

"Come in."

I took a breath and walked into Mr. Walsh's office. It was clean. No white covers to be seen.

Mr. Walsh sat in his chair.

He waved to the chair I'd sat in more that semester than I had in my entire time at Lupton.

"Mr. Walsh," I said, sitting. "I know you know, but I want to confess before—"

He waved a hand. I stopped.

"Sixty books were turned in," he said. "Sixty."

I nodded. "I know. That's why I want to take respon—"

He waved a hand again.

"Most of them had quotes on them," he said.

"Yes, but I don't think you should hunt down every person who wrote a quote. I was the one who put them up—"

He finally looked at me. "Ms. Evans, let me do the talking."

I bit my lip and then looked down at the chair. He stood, put his hands behind his back, and walked over to his window.

"Did you read any of those quotes, Ms. Evans?"

"All of them, sir."

"'I found bravery here' on a banned copy of *Speak* by

Laurie Halse Anderson. 'I have seen through another man's eyes, and I am changed forever' on a banned copy of *Don't Tread on Me* by Lukas Gebhardt. Then there's 'Someone remind me, going forward, to hug first and ask questions later' and 'This book reminded me to actually care about things. Thank you.'"

He paused, and then turned to me.

"And how do these quotes strike you?"

"I'm sorry, sir, I don't think I understand the question."

"Did they move you? Were they what made you decide to confess to running the library to a room full of Chattanooga movers and shakers? To a room filled with multiple members of the board of Lupton Academy? To jeopardize a potential college scholarship?"

"Sort of," I said. "I mean, yeah. In a way. A lot of things did. Mostly the fact that I was going to be expelled anyway. It wasn't that brave."

"Have you read *The Chocolate War*, Ms. Evans?" he asked, sitting back in his seat, this time holding my gaze.

"Not in a long time," I said.

"The book is prohibited media. In fact, I caught you walking in the halls with two copies of *The Chocolate War*.

If you're attempting to save some sort of face by saying you haven't read it recently, it isn't necessary."

"I honestly haven't reread that one yet, Mr. Walsh. You catching me with those copies was just unlucky because I was taking them from the library donations pile."

"Ms. Evans, why are you in my office?"

"Uh. Because I'm about to be expelled?"

"Yes, I've been directed to expel you. But my question still stands. Why are you in my office?"

I didn't say anything. I didn't have anything to say.

"I want you to go back to your locker and get your things."

There it was. I took a deep breath and closed my eyes, attempting to push the tears back. I heard Levi's and Joss's voices, telling me to look up. To look him in the eye. In a swell of volume, they were joined by LiQui. By Jack. By Ashton. By all the quotes on the white covers.

I opened my eyes and looked at Mr. Walsh. "Yes, sir."

"After you do that," he said, "I want you to go to class. I want you to study. And I want you to always answer yes."

I sat still. Not sure if he was joking.

"You want me to go to class?"

He nodded.

"You want me to study?"

He nodded.

"You want me to always answer yes?"

Again, he nodded.

"To what?"

He stood, walked over to the door, and opened it.

My heart beating fast, I grabbed my backpack and waited for him to answer.

"'Do I dare disturb the universe?'"

I stared at him. Had he read *The Chocolate War*? How did he know that quote?

He looked at me and nodded. "One last question, Ms. Evans."

I wiped a tear from my cheek. "Yes, Principal Walsh?"

"Was there a book that started all this?"

"*Don't Tread on Me* by Lukas Gebhardt."

He nodded. "I think I'd like to read it."

I smiled. "You should."

"You're going to be late to class."

"Thank you."

"No, thank you."

## ALL THE RIGHT FIRES

I walked toward the reopened library to find my friends. I followed my normal path, the one that'd take me past my locker, but it didn't seem that normal. It seemed . . . hopeful. Different in a way I couldn't describe. Like everything felt bigger than it had the last time I'd walked that path. The grandeur of second chances. The vistas of being sure of who you were and what you believed.

My locker came into view. I stopped in front of it and stared. Rehashing. Reliving. Rethinking.

My combination lock was gone, which was probably something that had happened after I left on Friday. I guessed I'd have to get a new one.

I swung the door open, ready to see a gray metal

emptiness instead of a vast wall of white.

But.

Covered banned books took up the whole space.

Stacked from the bottom of my locker to the top.

Only one copy stood on its ends, and it was wrapped in white construction paper.

On the front, a quote:

*I'm sorry, Jerry.*
*—Brother Leon*

Principal Walsh.

I could only guess it was one of the copies of *The Chocolate War* he'd taken from me a few weeks ago. Had he picked it up to read it then? Or had he read it when he was younger? Maybe he'd decided he wanted to be a school administrator because of it. Maybe he'd started his career with the goal of keeping any school he touched from becoming the school in *The Chocolate War*, and somewhere along the way he got lost. Maybe this whole incident had brought him back. Reminded him.

I remembered the look he'd given the banned copies

when he took them from me in his office.

He'd remembered. I didn't know what he'd remembered, but it had been enough to bring me here, in front of this locker.

Did the board know he was doing this? Did Mrs. Lodenhauer know? I shook my head. No. When I was in his office, he'd said, "I've been directed to expel you," but . . . he hadn't. He'd have to face whiplash when the board found out I was still here. But the board didn't walk the halls. He did. Was that why he was giving me back the white covers? Did he want me to keep going? Was this book code for "rebuild"?

There was only one way to find out.

I grabbed a copy of *Don't Tread on Me* I still had in my backpack, and then grabbed the copy of *The Chocolate War* Principal Walsh had wrapped. I ran back to his office and knocked on the door. He was there.

"Yes, Ms. Evans?" he said.

I walked in, holding out *Don't Tread on Me*. "You said you think you'd like to read this?"

When I'd started the Unlib, I'd been afraid that books couldn't do the things I thought they could. But there I stood, handing a banned book to the same person who'd made me question them in the first place, believing in them even more than I had before.

In those seconds, it felt like all the words and magic in the universe converged right where I stood, telling me the told and untold stories of bravery, strength, hope, and hurt. Whispering in my ears that there were still so many books, choices, and changes that hadn't yet dared to disturb the universe.

## GOODBYE, LUPTON ACADEMY

It was May.

I'd survived.

I wasn't afraid.

Not of books, at least.

Dying of heatstroke before I could even have a day not owned by a school?

Yes.

Of that, I was certainly afraid.

I sat, covered in long black gross sticky graduation-gown fabric. To my left, LiQui. To her left, Resi Alistair. To my right, Ashton. To Ashton's right, Jack. We were sweating out all the knowledge we'd learned since freshman year, sitting in a bunch of stickier nylon chairs on the football field (the SPA expansion would bring a much-needed auditorium). Parents surrounded us on the bleachers where we'd once sat. Where LiQui and I had sat for four years. Where Ashton and I had had our first conversation. Where Jack and I had eaten three bags of Twizzlers.

Principal James Willings stood in front of a podium on a small elevated stage up front, reading out name after name with his deep rumble of a voice. When a name was given, the correct student would move out from waiting in the wings and begin their walk across the stage to grab a tiny rolled-up piece of paper with nothing written on it. While they were walking, the new principal's assistant would read a small snippet about what that student was going to do next.

Principal James Willings was obviously not the same person as Principal Milton Walsh.

The day after Principal Walsh refused to expel me, he resigned. He didn't even give his two weeks' notice; he just left. The day after that, Ms. Croft's story broke on the front page of the local paper, the *Chattanooga Times Free Press*: "Lupton Academy Teacher Fired for Raising Questions About School's Banned-Book Policy."

The article pretty much outlined everything Ms. Croft had told us at Queso, with a special guest appearance by "former principal Milton Walsh" in which he confirmed that the board, indeed, had directed him to fire her. Apparently, he was done playing Lupton's—or, rather, the Lodenhauers'—games.

NPR picked up the story. After that? CNN. Then suddenly Lupton Academy was everywhere. Being pushed by all sides to reform. And for a month or two, the Unlib I'd rebuilt swelled. Students who hadn't wanted anything to do with me the first go-round were suddenly checking books out. Things seemed like they were going to change. The student body as a whole started to push back. LiQui led the charge. Administration kept saying things like "We're reconsidering the policy" or "We're reviewing it during our next board meeting."

But . . . they never did.

All they did was shuffle people around. Switch out board members for relatives.

As of the day before graduation, the mention of "prohibited media" still remained in the student handbook.

Resi walked back down our aisle, back from getting her nothing diploma. It seemed like we'd been here for ages, but we were only halfway through the *B*s. The Mav had just crossed the stage, and Ashton was on deck. Leave it to pre-heatstroke and extreme boredom to make you realize how many friends you had in the first ten letters of the alphabet.

I leaned my head back, trying to regulate my temperature from surface-of-the-sun down to Hot-Pocket-just-out-of-the-microwave, when I felt a plastic bag press against my arm. I looked down and saw Jack holding on to a giant family-size bag of Twizzlers.

"Eat them while Ashton is up there. That way you can actually enjoy them."

"You're living in his house now," LiQui pointed out. "You should be giving him first dibs."

I laughed, grabbed two out of the bag, and passed them down to Resi and LiQui.

"How's that going, Jack?" I asked. "Ashton a good roomie?"

"Literally the best. Coming out for real has been the best thing that has ever happened to me. The Brickses aren't trying to bleach me clean. I feel like I can breathe."

The second Jack Lodenhauer came back from Parkview Mental Health Center, he came out to every friend who didn't know. This, of course, spread. Quickly. For a minute, people cared, and it was the talk of the town, but then some moved on. Some didn't. But they weren't, for the most part, people who loved him. All his friends? They stayed. I stayed. We stayed.

Jack's family? They were in the category of those who didn't move on. In fact, they hadn't talked to him since. Emerson texted Jack every once in a while, but word was that if Jack replied, Emerson would delete it from his inbox because he was terrified of what his parents would do if they found out.

"'I found bravery here,'" I said, pointing at him.

He nodded, looked at his shoes, then smiled. "I know."

I looked back at the podium.

Resi leaned over LiQui, tapped me on the leg, and asked, "Are you okay?"

I nodded. "Yeah. I am. Seriously. I wanted you to take it, remember? We went through all this yesterday. We don't have to rehash it again."

She looked down at her feet. "Yeah, I . . . You deserved it. Not me."

"Res, you know I love you, but that is the truth," LiQui added.

I shrugged. "So I didn't get the Founders Scholarship, but I did get a little bit of money from it. I've been accepted to Vandy. I've got the summer to figure out how to make it work."

"Well, you don't have to figure it out alone," Resi said.

"Word," LiQui added. "Maybe you and I can split the cash my grandparents are going to give me."

I rolled my eyes. "LiQui, they finally agreed to pay for your POTUS degree and now you're going to split it?"

She shrugged. "What? We're roommates, Clara. Roommates. I don't wanna live with some girl whose favorite band is Jason Mraz and 'just can't believe the college won't let me light incense in the room. It's my room.' I'd kill her. No lie. I'm not even going to leave it up to chance."

"What if I told you I've recently gotten into incense?"

She held up a hand. "Don't play that game. Quit."

"Well," Resi said, leaning back in her chair, "we'll figure something out."

"Ashton Bricks!" Principal Willings yelled, and we jumped out of our chairs and cheered as loud as a thunderstorm—so loud that we missed his "what they're doing next" section.

LiQui stood. "A round of queso on me if I trip on that

stage. I've been practicing my walk in these heels for months. Witness me." She walked toward the stage.

More names. More people. I was too distracted by being here. By being in the chair next to my friends. By the heat, but, if I really dug deep, I knew I was thankful for the heat too. Because that meant I'd made it. Even though Principal Walsh had let me go, once he left, I worried the board would make the new principal finish the job. I mean, Janet Lodenhauer was highly involved in the school and she wanted me dead. Not just gone. But . . . nothing ever came of it. After Christmas break came and went and I was still walking back into LA, I realized that I was going to stay. I think, after Ms. Croft broke the story, they knew that if they did anything to me, it'd bring even more negative press.

So . . . I finished the semester.

LiQui stepped on the stage. I wanted a tiny trip. A tiny one. It could even be that her heel got stuck in the carpet so I could argue technicality. I loved LiQui. But queso was on the line.

"LiQuiana Carson!"

LiQui started across the stage and we all stood and screamed, "Queen Li!"

The principal's assistant's mousy voice cut through our applause. "LiQuiana plans to eat queso with her friends for the rest of the summer and will then attend Vanderbilt to earn a bachelor's degree in political science."

"I like incense!" I yelled as loud as I could.

In the middle of a step, LiQui bent forward and let out a laugh. Her heel wobbled—very slightly, but it was a wobble I'd fight to the death for. She straightened herself up quick, grabbed the diploma, and hurried across the stage.

I chanted, "Queso, queso, queso," as she walked back to her seat.

More names. More heat. More sticky graduating.

Finally, my name was announced, and you would've thought the LA Vols had just scored a Super Bowl. Tears pushed against my eyes, but then I laughed when I thought about Janet Lodenhauer's face souring somewhere in the bleachers. I stepped onto the stage, my heart a nearly audible thud. My hands shaking. Everyone kept cheering, and I couldn't help but turn and look at the hundreds of students in front of me.

Maybe the applause made me feel incredibly awkward. And maybe I created a reason that people were applauding to make it feel less awkward, but I didn't think so. I believed that the applause wasn't for me, strictly speaking. It was for books.

I clapped too. It probably looked weird, a girl clapping for herself, but I couldn't not join in.

Books are a light. A light that melts ignorance and hate. They show new paths to take. Or, for some, the depth of seemingly unfixable brokenness. Books illuminate something different for all of us. Books change lives because they're matches, starting fires that show the grandness of the world, the depth of others, a path for us to see ourselves.

Such fires might come easy.

They might come hard.

They might make us stronger.

They might cost us and the people around us.

They might make us braver.

They might make us disagree.

They might make us closer.

They might make us offended.

They might make us happy.

They might make someone hurt.

They might make us overconfident.

They might make us confused.

They might make us think we know more than we do.

But they will make us free.

And I longed for the world to continue to spin in their glow.

I'd always fight for people to have the choice to be surrounded by that glow.

But even more than that?

I'd always fight for a world that continued to be recipients of books such as those.

Of such fires.

## A LEGACY OF DOMINOES

I was at Mojo with the crew, fresh out of my grad gear and stuffing a burrito in my face like a barn resident, when Emerson Lodenhauer came up to our table.

Jack gave him a timid "Hey."

I couldn't get a read on the situation. Were they congenial? Were they enemies? Were they nothing? Last I'd heard, Emerson was barely talking to Jack.

Emerson looked at me. "Clara, can I talk to you?"

The question took me by surprise, mostly because I'd never, not even once, talked to Emerson Lodenhauer, nor even been less than twenty feet from him.

I cast an *uhhh?* glance at Jack.

Jack nodded.

I stood up from the table and followed Emerson to the outside porch, to the table farthest away from people.

He held out his hand. "I'm Emerson."

"I'm Clara."

"I know."

"Yeah. I bet you do." I paused, realizing how dumb that sounded. "I mean, not that I think I'm awesome, or something. It was just because of, like, your mom hating my guts. Or whatever. And the whole . . . your brother situation. No, that's not what I mean. I'm just saying that your family and I have history and—"

He looked at Jack through a window; then, thank God, Emerson interrupted my panic talking. "I want to take over the library. I want to run the Unlib."

I stared at him for a moment, laughed, then put an arm around his shoulder and smiled. "Well, well, well. Will the dominoes ever stop falling?"

He cocked his head, confused.

"You'll see," I said. "You'll see."

## THE END

## ACKNOWLEDGMENTS

Writing this book was really really really really really really hard. Possibly the hardest creative thing I've ever done, and I owe so so much to so many people for helping me survive it. By no means is this an exhaustive list, for it takes a universe to write a book.

The OG Clara: This book wouldn't exist without you. When I was going to quit writing, you said, "I think you can do it. I think we can work it out." I can't even begin to put into words how much all your love, understanding, sacrifice, and encouragement kept me alive and afloat the last few years. This is *our* book. I love you.

Asa: It's a different book, but you are *still* enough. I love you, bud. It's an honor to be your dad, and I'm excited that I get to do it for the rest of my life.

Emmie: You are a ray of sun. I love you, and I'm so happy I get to write your name in my books now.

Mom: Thanks for raising me around books and bringing me to the library when I was little. Also, thanks for not being afraid of overdue fines.

Dad: I love you. I miss you. I hope you know that.

Demaster Crew: Thanks for your constant support of me and for not telling Clara to run away because she wanted to marry a writer.

Charlie: Thanks for always understanding, for making jokes when things are hard, and being encouraging at the same time. Oh, and for being excited about my book news even when you have no idea what I'm talking about.

Caroline: Thanks for your friendship, and keeping me fresh and looking like a whole snack.

JM & Andrew: Thanks for all your support and non-stop love. Let's go get some mango margs, PLZ.

Matt and Crystal: Y'all's support and friendship means the world to me. Thank you. Oh, FYI, I'm not saying you need to buy six copies of this book like you did for *TOA* in order to keep up your #1 fan status, but it wouldn't hurt your ranking.

Eric Smith: We've been waiting for this one. Thank you for loving this book so much that you wanted to chill with me for four-plus years to get it published. Here's to more books. Also, don't worry, I'll wait at least a day after this comes out to send you my *so now what do we do?* message.

Claudia, Stephanie, and the Katherine Tegen team: Thanks for believing in this book and me. Thanks × 1000 for not freaking out when I sent you that first rewrite. That thing was horrible. Your patience with and kindness to me while I struggled through this book mean the world to me. Thank you for giving me this chance. Join me for a moment of silence for all the characters who died in the making of this book. RIP Topher, Chris, Tali, Darius, Mandy, Joshua, Max (Clara's younger brother), Andy Alskez, Louie Alskez, and Mr. Ricardo.

C.J. Redwine: You are a light. I'm so glad I know you and that I get to write books/live life with someone as fantastic as you. Thank you for always saying, "You can do it. You'll get through it."

Matt Landis: I hate you.

Latt Mandis: Like Jesus came out of Nazareth, you came out of Twitter. I'm so thankful for you.

Adam Sass and Matthew Hubbard: Thanks for being willing to tell me if I was being a horrible human being. This book wouldn't be what it is without your insight, care, and hard-earned wisdom. I'm honored to know the both of you, and I'm so excited to watch you both slay publishing.

Carlos: Thanks for all your detention advice.

Librarians, teachers, educators: I am in constant awe of your service. Thank you.

Todd Bol: Clara's Tiny Little Libraries were totally inspired by you and your amazing work. I am and will continue to be thankful for the movement you started with Little Free Libraries, for your undying commitment to getting such fires into the hands of the people who need them. You will be missed.

Glen Cole, Katie McGarry, Brian McClard, Thomas Hayes, David Norman, the Rock Creek Youth Group, David Arnold: Whether it was answering my random nit-picky *how does this work in real life* questions, giving me plot advice, unknowingly giving me conflict ideas, or just being encouraging, this book wouldn't be the same without you.

Jesus: Thanks for giving me the words to write, for letting me share them, and for putting all the names I wrote above into my life. Please let your goodness and gospel shine through these words.